advance praise for
HYBRID HEART

"Kusano pulls no punches in this portrayal of a ro............. industry, where an idol's privacy is violated with technology until one has to wonder just how much of themselves they are willing to lose in order to achieve their artistic goals. Touching on themes of self-acceptance, friendship, and reclaiming your own artistic agency, *Hybrid Heart* will move you like only your favorite song can, by leaving you a sobbing mess."
—Francesca Tacchi, author of *Let the Mountains Be My Grave*

"Never has the Faustian bargain been so corporeally rendered as in the glossy, ruthless *Hybrid Heart*. Kusano paints a high wire portrait of a talented singer making herself into a candy-colored ghost. By turns wryly incisive and emotionally devastating, Kusano creates an unflinching world where the demands of the idol machine are as simple as they are severe: give us everything, or you will be nothing."
—Bendi Barrett, author of *Empire of the Feast*

"Lavish and claustrophobic, *Hybrid Heart* ruthlessly scrutinizes its pop idol protagonist's world as she turns that same scrutiny on herself, her dwindling choices, her compressed life, and slowly reclaims her dreams from the nightmare they've become."
—Kat Weaver, co-author of *Uncommon Charm*

"Iori Kusano's *Hybrid Heart* is a story of fame and deep, abiding loneliness. It defies expectations and offers us exactly what we need. Kusano's prose is gorgeous, precise, and controlled. Their great gift is to show us what lies beneath the lure of fame and the policing of female-assigned bodies, to reveal, with perfect tenderness and unflinching honesty, the scars, the blood, the imperfect, essential core. *Hybrid Heart* may break yours—or resuscitate it."
—Izzy Wasserstein, author of *All the Hometowns You Can't Stay Away From*

"*Hybrid Heart* is a gorgeously rendered story about power, control, and breaking yourself out of a cage made out of false dreams. Kusano slams the reader right into the messy heart of the idol industry and then surgically proceeds to rip the reader's own heart open."
—Isabel J. Kim, Shirley Jackson Award-winning author

"Shimmering, crystallised paranoia. *Idolmaster* meets *Perfect Blue* in this stunning tale of panic-infused pop. Kusano is one to watch out for."
—Vina Jie-Min Prasad, Nebula, Hugo, Sturgeon & Locus-nominated author

Neon Hemlock Press
www.neonhemlock.com
@neonhemlock

© 2022 Iori Kusano

Hybrid Heart
Iori Kusano

Cover Illustration by Natsujurishi
Cover/Interior Design by dave ring
Edited by dave ring

Print ISBN-13: 978-1-952086-58-8
Ebook ISBN-13: 978-1-952086-65-6

NEON HEMLOCK

Iori Kusano
HYBRID HEART

Neon Hemlock Press

THE 2023 NEON HEMLOCK NOVELLA SERIES

Hybrid Heart

BY IORI KUSANO

to 윤트, who didn't realize that teenage girls grow up, get therapy, and get mad 🙂

壱

HER HAIR MOVES like it's real, and Rei hates her for it.

Digital idols were clunky when the technology was new. Their hair clipped through their arms or swayed in one solid mass. But every strand of LYRICO's hair appears to move on its own, to flutter and bend and slide just like the real thing.

Rei should have been asleep hours ago. Instead, she engages in revenge bedtime procrastination worthy of a student before midterms, beaming music videos directly into her own head via NeuroDouga. It's a little after three in the morning, or 27:00 in the cant of night owls and pleasure seekers—she can tell by the noise of people leaving the bar across the street. If she stretched out her mind a little into her server uplink she'd be told the exact time down to the second, instant as thought, but she doesn't want to know. It's going to be a pain spackling over her tired panda eyes tomorrow to hide them from her fans. She needs her beauty sleep. Kosaka will know exactly how late she stayed up, even though she turned out the smart lights hours ago. She bets he can pull her NeuroDouga search history, timestamps and all. It's her old personal account, from way back before she joined

Hiyoko PRO, but she wouldn't put it past him to have breached it.

The next video recommended for her is a deep cut from LYRICO's back catalog, one of those B-sides that only the hardcore fans dig. Rei queues it up.

▶

HIYOKO PRO HAS its very own seven story building in a glossy, gentrified corner of Shinagawa; that's how people know it matters. The lobby is full of real plants all lush and green and the elevators move in perfect silence. But the building is between an upscale yakiniku restaurant and a Michelin-starred noodle shop. Mornings are fine, but in the evening the smells of cooking always get into the air conditioning and remind Rei of how hungry she is. She hurries herself through the plush lobby and up to the fourth floor so that no one could ever accuse her of lingering.

This level of the office is open and bright, each desk facing a black leather couch, each couch flanked by a tall potted plant. It's not as cramped as the third-floor bullpen, packed full of newer hires, but nowhere near as nice as the private offices upstairs.

Of course Kosaka is at his desk by the window, in a rumpled suit, tie already loosened. His black hair stands up in stiff clumps. The reflection of his computer screen blanks out his eyes behind his glasses. Maybe he never went home last night. Rei knows that he stays over in the office sometimes. The scent of his cologne has permanently soaked into the leather couch their visitors wait on.

"Did you see the rankings?" he asks, not looking up from his computer.

She had. LYRICO had blown past her on the charts with a new song that AventureP uploaded only that morning. She decides to pretend it doesn't matter.

"Whatever," she says, full of bravado. "'Miracle ♡ Heartscape' is a month old. It was going to fall off the top five anyway. We're about to start the next promotion cycle, so let's focus on that. Every step takes us closer to the Budokan, right? And then to the Tokyo Dome."

It takes a real effort to keep from freezing as she waits for him to react, forcing herself to pop a pod in the coffeemaker without watching him. She thinks she's playing this one right, giving him the brisk, businesslike Rei instead of the one who commiserates and fawns, but she's gotten it wrong before.

He is silent as the coffeemaker grinds and whirs. Then, just as its hurgling peaks, he says, "You're right."

The coffee trickles into the algal polyfoam cup in her hand. Rei keeps her back very, very straight and doesn't turn around, not until Kosaka finally says, "Nothing to do but keep pushing. We can knock that doll off the charts."

The dispenser in Kosaka's shoulder crunches, just audible under the bubbling of the air conditioner, as he triggers a dose of Pacifix. She doubts it's his first today, but that's none of Rei's business, except for the times it is, except for the times he makes it her business—

But he is a respected manager at Hiyoko PRO, a top seller. He produced Yukarin, who'd won three Excellent Work awards and a Grand Prix at the Japan Record Awards in under five years, with a Gold Disc and two Kōhaku Uta Gassen appearances to boot. More importantly, when the order came down from the CEO's office to axe Venus Versus, Kosaka had believed in her enough to carry her forward as a solo act. His hard work had boosted her to the escape velocity necessary to leave Ririko's scandal behind. He'd shed furious tears when Ririko's face was splashed across Sunday Photo and a half dozen other webloids, then dunked his head in the bathroom sink, but when Rei hauled him back by the collar of his jacket, he shook the water out of his hair, took three doses of Pacifix, and gave her a new song.

Iori Kusano

She used to be effortlessly grateful for this. Now she dredges her gratitude every day from the deep well of memory and hopes Kosaka doesn't notice the difference.

Rei grabs a chair from the desk next to his and wheels it to his side, curling into it. She sips her coffee, watching Kosaka over the rim of her cup. This is an image easier to evoke in autumn, sweater weather and no sweat pooling at the small of her back, but she can make it work like this too: slim and cool in capris and a linen button-down over a tank top, plasma-permed curls spilling over her shoulders, her heart-shaped face framed by curls of coffee steam. The important thing is ensuring that Kosaka will look up and see her big, trusting, sympathetic eyes—exactly what he likes best. She thinks of this version of herself as Soft Café Nymphette. Sad boys love Soft Café Nymphette and how she smiles enigmatically over her coffee.

Her circle lenses itch something awful but she cannot risk blinking yet. Kosaka looks up and rewards her with a weary smile. "Well, Top-Idol-to-Be. Do you want to hear what gems I'll add to your crown today?"

That's one of the frustrating things about her job. Rei isn't allowed to know in advance what shape her day will take beyond the barest details. If she knew, she could plan, and poor disgraced Ririko, once the other half of Venus Versus, has shown what mischief idols make if they have even a little power to plan. They can slip away, meet people, fall in love.

And idols are absolutely not allowed to fall in love. It's right there in the contract.

Kosaka plucks the cup of coffee from her hands and takes a long sip himself, even though the one on his desk is still steaming. Rei is still smiling adoringly when he returns it to her.

"Tell me," she bubbles at him, twirling a dyed-brown curl around one finger, hating herself a little bit more for playing this game.

THE ANIMATE IN Akihabara might not, all things
considered, be an optimal location for a handshake event.
It's cramped and warm no matter the time of day, with
narrow aisles and tight, humid staircases. But it's where
Rei's fans have assembled to meet her and pick up their
pre-ordered copies of her newest single, so here she is.

"Stars in Monochrome" is four minutes and thirteen
seconds long, and starts from the hook, though Rei
personally believes the pre-chorus, swelling like a cold
wave, is the best part. It is her fifth single since she went
solo fourteen months ago, and the second-cour ED song
for *Entropy Fighter Mizuki*. The B-side is called "MIRROR
FRACTURE." It is three minutes and nineteen seconds
long, and will be played in its entirety as an insert song
during episode twenty-three, when Entropy Fighter
Mizuki will sacrifice her identity and re-emerge in a new
body drawn by an entirely different character designer.
The production team predicts that this choice will
polarize the fanbase but ultimately serve the direction and
creative vision of *Mizuki*.

Rei has not seen the anime beyond the clips she's been
shown when she records Mizuki's singing voice. All of
Entropy Fighter Mizuki's spoken lines are handled by
a real voice actress, a pro with a ten-year filmography
behind her. If anyone tries to discuss the latest episodes
today she'll laugh and say she's saving it up to binge when
she can get time off.

She only has idle intentions of watching *Entropy Fighter
Mizuki*. There are a lot of other things she wants to see
first. But certain polite fictions are necessary, when so
much of her fanbase loves her for being Mizuki. She
doesn't want to think about how many of them only listen
to her because of *Mizuki*, or how many might leave her
when the series ends. Will she have to keep trotting out

these same songs for the rest of her career, just to keep them hooked?

Kosaka herds her to the fourth floor and behind a table. A small legion of shop staff opens crates nearby. Like most artists, her music is mostly sold via direct neural download, but customers who pre-ordered were entered in a raffle for tickets to the handover event. Every pre-order customer gets a swag bag, and 250 of them will have theirs personally handed to them by Rei instead of receiving it by mail.

The swag bag contains: a can badge featuring the cover art for "Stars in Monochrome," an acrylic keyholder, a penlight that slowly pulses its way through every shade of blue in the hex chart, a plastic pouch of blue and white konpeito, one of eight collectable bromides, and a lanyard. It seems generous, but the manufacturing cost of a few thousand units of cheap plastic crap is low, and its perceived value and rarity pushes pre-orders.

"We should have raised the cap to five hundred," Kosaka mutters in her ear. "It'd look better to have the line out the door and down the block."

It's not that Rei dislikes handover events, precisely. It's just that face-to-face interaction collapses the distance between idol and fan to something uncomfortably close. Rei knows that this kind of warm interpersonal connection is her last remaining advantage over digital idols, but two hundred and fifty people are a lot to talk to individually. She'd prefer to address them collectively, from the stage or by broadcasting into the comfortingly formless void of the internet.

She doesn't mind being perceived but there's something viscerally upsetting about watching others perceive her. It's one thing to know abstractly that the audience is judging her, and another, significantly worse thing to watch them do it in real time. Can't she just perform in the vague direction of the collective blob?

"Doing okay, Rei?" Kosaka asks.

She throws him an artificially bright smile over her shoulder. "What are you talking about? I'm in top form today!"

And she turns her focus back to the gathering crowd. In their array of glasses and masks and caps they are faceless to her, but she pretends to know them. A wave here, a smile there, and she projects her voice all the way to the back of the room—which is not far at all.

"Hiiii! I'm so happy you all came out to meet me today, and to celebrate my new single. I see a lot of familiar faces here and a lot of new ones too. Whether you've been my fan for a long time, or you're just meeting me now, I'm really grateful for your support.

"I'd also like to say thank you to Director Suzuki and Music Supervisor Iwabuchi for asking me to sing for *Entropy Fighter Mizuki*. Being part of this show has been such a special experience for me, and I'll always carry Mizuki in my heart. I've had so many wonderful things happen in my life since I became an idol, but being able to meet my fans as Mizuki is the best of all."

She's saying everything she's supposed to. The packed crowd nods along, applauding. And then Kosaka signals one of the shop staff to unhook the restraining cable. The line unspools towards her. Panic arcs white through her brain and Rei pins her smile to her face like a butterfly under glass.

They are here to see her. They are happy to see her. She should not want to flee. But there are days when every eye on her is a needle in her tender skin, and today is one of them.

"Rei, I'm so happy I got to meet you!"

"I came all the way from Osaka to see you!"

"Congratulations on your new single!"

"Your new costume really suits you! You look just like Mizuki!"

"I'll always cheer you on!"

Rei is outside herself, watching from somewhere very far away as she clasps a parade of hands: sweaty, clammy, soft, calloused. She smiles with her glossy little mouth and throws peace signs and blows kisses for photos, dainty and immaculate in her tulle-and-mycopleather minidress, long thin legs made longer still with high-heeled boots. This ease and grace isn't in her character; some whim of genetics deprived her of it, or at least that's her best guess. She knows—Kosaka has told her—that she must be grateful for their eyes. How will she know she's lovely unless someone is generous enough to tell her?

There can be no merit in a vacuum. Without other idols to outstrip, without eyes to judge them all, she cannot know her own value.

"You were better when you were in V²."

The distance between Rei-on-autopilot and Rei-observing collapses, abruptly and unpleasantly.

"I still like your music," her fan says. He's tall, reedy, staring intently from behind his round glasses. "But you shouldn't have dumped Ririko. You were better together."

He's not wrong, the vicious lurking grief inside hisses. Rei is shaking. She opens her mouth and nothing comes out, not even the agreement trying to push its way up her throat. The walled city of Yoshizawa Rei is falling.

And then Kosaka is there, shoving forward to get between her and the table, making himself a shield. The bergamot in the cologne Rei bought him for his birthday fills her nose and binds to her GPCRs. He is solid. She is safe.

"Rei will be taking a brief break," he announces.

He puts a hand on the small of her back and guides her back towards the employee breakroom. Rei keeps her smile firmly fixed in place. Fifteen meters until she can let it slip. Ten. Five. Here, here, she's safe now—

The door shuts behind them and Kosaka bursts into tears, utterly preempting Rei's own upset.

Indignation wells up in Rei; she fights down the urge to stamp her foot—*no, no, this isn't about you! I'm the one who should be crying, because I'm small and mean and cowardly and even a total stranger can see it!*

Instead she puts her hands on his shoulders, electric blue nitrogel nails vivid against his gray suit. She smoothes his lapels, straightens his tie, plucks the handkerchief from his breast pocket to dab at his dark, dewy eyes.

"Shh-shh, shh-shh," she hums to the person whose entire job is taking care of her. "Shh, we're okay, we're just fine. We need to get back out there and finish greeting everyone."

"How dare he," Kosaka whispers, nearly choking on his sniffles. "Ririko betrayed our dream. Ririko betrayed all our hard work—"

Ririko didn't betray her. Ririko loved someone enough to shield herself. She carved out a piece of her life and declared it off-limits to their company and their fans. The same Ririko who moved like her skeleton was trying to shake its meat glove off, who projected an interiority that locked the audience out, who sang with intensity unseemly for an idol.

If anything, Rei is the traitor here. Rei stood aside and let Kosaka discard her best friend and the dream they shared over a rule that shouldn't have been imposed on her in the first place. Rei agreed that idols were public property. Rei dropped her best friend like deadweight, told the webloids how sad she was, and then went onstage alone to make herself over into everyone's favorite, despite the fact that Ririko was a better singer than Rei by every metric.

"Kosaka," she says quietly. "Kosaka, I have to go meet my fans. Do you need to take your Pacifix? Will that help?"

His wide, flat nostrils flare. He straightens up

incrementally, shoulders still shaking. "No. Go do your job," he says, but some instinct warns her that she'll be punished later for leaving him here. She is not supposed to walk away until he is ready to let her. But Rei feels another flash of rage, burning up from her gut and threatening to burst from her glossed lips: *This isn't your sorrow. You don't grieve this, you don't feel guilty for it—you're only sorry someone reminded you of it.*

Rei straightens her spine and walks back onto the shop floor alone.

THE FIRST TIME Rei went onstage without Ririko she was so charged with terror that her body put itself on autopilot, some hindbrain prey drive protecting her. She didn't even remember the show afterwards. The memory simply hadn't been saved to disk. What she has of it now is all secondhand, gleaned from the videos Kosaka uploaded to her NeuroDouga channel.

The camera was far enough from the stage that she can't tell on the feed whether she trembled. The fans cheered and clapped, chanting the standard mix: "Tiger, Fire, Cyber, Fiber, Diver, Viber, jaa-jaa!" She watched herself slough off her fear and stack her vertebrae back up, gathering strength from that stream of nonsense, a rope tossed into her grasping hand.

And she sang.

Only when it was over did Rei realize that she'd sweated through the back of her top, that a blister had bloomed on her left heel where one boot rubbed wrong, that she'd shed nearly a third of her eyelash extensions. She couldn't register any of those things in the moment, but here was the evidence of her efforts.

The second time was worse. She was there for it.

She shook so hard that everyone could see it. Her teeth

chattered so loudly that the mic picked it up. She felt every drop of sweat beading on her shoulders.

And the crowd was silent. Rei recalled the stories of rejected idols facing down black oceans, and wondered whether she was about to meet one.

Just when she thought she might flee the stage, having forgotten the words to even introduce herself or greet the crowd, having forgotten everything but sheer animal terror—

Kosaka started the music, and the music saved her. Rei might forget empty words and niceties, but she never forgets lyrics.

After the show, floundering in the adrenaline hangover, words deserted her again. There was nothing to distract her from the high keening of her loneliness but Kosaka crowing over her victory.

"We're better off without her," he said, and Rei pretended to believe him.

弍

IT IS NOT precisely accurate to say that Rei doesn't leave her house for the next two days.

She wastes her precious Sunday off: a rare treat—or half of one, anyway, since Kosaka scheduled a salon appointment and half an hour at the tenteki bar for her—squandered by staring at the ceiling, counting the sirens she can hear through her thin walls, and succumbing to the invisible weight sitting on her chest. She doesn't even make herself sit up to test her voice on a scale or two. Can't, won't, whichever. Does it matter? When Kosaka calls to ask why she missed her hair appointment, she pleads a migraine, whispering that she can't bear light or noise. There's a long pause, and she knows he's checking the sensors embedded in her futon via its connected app, verifying that she hasn't budged from it all day. At last he grudgingly agrees that she seems unwell and tells her to sleep it off "until her neurohumors rebalance themselves." She thinks this is an unscientific instruction at best, but she's neither well-educated nor energetic enough to dispute it.

Her wanton disobedience ought to provoke some feeling in her, excitement or shame or fear of punishment, but all she feels is numb. She falls asleep sometime during the hazy hours of counting the flecks of static on the inside of her eyelids.

It takes Rei approximately four hours of effort on Monday to peel herself out of the futon. Eventually she chucks her pillow across the room to force herself up. She skips the shower, struggles into an oversized hoodie and shorts, crams her curls into a cap, obscures her face with one of the special nanite masks that filter out the city smog and shield her from easy recognition.

The conbini is less than one hundred meters from her building's door and every step feels like she's trudging through a pool of jelly. Summer has burst on Tokyo like a watermelon dropped on the sidewalk. The humid air pushes back against her, presses in from all sides, and she sweats under her hoodie.

Lectro-ads flash in the conbini windows, cycling through commercials, and when hers comes up Rei's own face stares back at her, pink-lipped and dewy, blowing kisses with both hands and tracing hearts in the air with a slender finger.

Rei is sure that her real fingers are not that slim. Her idol, idolized, ideal self, the one she sees winking from pachinko machines and giant screens, is infinitely lighter than the real thing.

Inside Lawson the air conditioning is set to "arctic" and Rei finds herself shivering as she piles the cheap pudding of self-pity into her plastic basket. She will pay for this later; she knows from experience the storm of guilt trips and recriminations that Kosaka will whip up if she weighs in a fraction over her perfect 43 kilos. Maybe her period would even come back—wouldn't that be funny? But she is too hollow to care right now.

What would it feel like, Rei wonders, if she just didn't try so hard all the time? What if she was just a person in the world?

But Rei is an idol and in order to remain one she will chisel away at herself until she's chipped to nothing, until she's only data and dust. This is not the worst thing to be.

She could, after all, be a person in the world: ordinary, unpublicized, obscure and unloved. Wouldn't that be worse—to know that she is exactly as small as she feels?

Back at home, Rei considers this as she pumps her brain full of LYRICO's voice, eats three pudding cups in a row, gives herself a stomachache, and ignores the blood sugar alert and the calorie intake meter pinging their warnings through her body. It's Hiyoko PRO wetware, a bioapp Kosaka had the company's occupational physician install. Even before Rei became an idol, every woman she knew was planning a diet or actively on one, no matter how slim they were. The tech just makes it easier to perfect herself. Deprivation makes her lovable; nourishing herself is monstrous.

LYRICO is a familiar lullaby now, her voice burrowing deep into Rei's skull. Something in that timbre reminds her of Ririko. Is it how her *oh* soars and echoes in the cathedral of her mouth, the *ah* that shoots straight from the top of her skull?

"We're like dolls," Ririko had laughed backstage, spinning so that her skirt flew. "Puppets, painted and dressed up and dancing."

Rei had thought so too, and reveled in it: the joyful relief of giving up control, of throwing herself to the whim of something bigger. She'd been too delighted to realize that Ririko wasn't having fun anymore. They'd spent years sharing everything even before they became idols, from erasers and battered manga to lipsticks and jackets. Why, then, would Rei ever have expected their feelings to diverge? They'd always shared those too. Their heartbeats had thumped along in sync for so long that Rei didn't notice they'd begun to slide out of time. If she was happy, surely Ririko must be, too.

Maybe Ririko and LYRICO don't sound alike at all. Maybe memory, the faulty data storage inherent to meat, is failing her. It's been so long since she heard Ririko sing.

Rei doesn't listen to their old recordings anymore or watch the shaky videos taken in dark underground venues. She's probably forgotten, she's probably just projecting—

She needs to get out of her own head. Time for some fan-subsidized distraction. Rei plucks blindly at the stack of gift cards on her nightstand. She grabs the first one that stays in her hand, scratches the flaky peel off to reveal the serial number.

Rei is discomfited at times by how deeply the internet has penetrated her body since becoming an idol. Nearly everyone uses neural streaming for entertainment—what better way to block out the unwelcome stimulus of the real world?—but from the day she signed her contract she has been in a perpetual state of transmission, uploading biodata to the Hiyoko PRO servers. She has forgotten how to truly disconnect, even when she wants to.

This is one of the tasks she still uses a device for. Rei needs steps between the jolt of an impulse and its fulfillment, places at which she can turn back, make better choices. So she keeps shopping apps out of her body. It'd be too risky to shop directly from her own brain; her finances are tight enough without the temptation. Likewise, Rei doesn't have social media extensions, even though they're getting popular with people her age—too easy to give in to recklessness.

Rei fumbles through her tangled blankets until she finds her smart. Kosaka has recently installed an app that lets him send emails and pings directly, without the intermediary of a smart. It's still in beta, which is the only reason he hasn't forced it into her head yet. She dismisses the notifications from Kosaka's pings. She can tell from the preview snippets he's scolding her for the pudding, and if she has to read even one line about how a pretty girl like Rei should take better care of herself, she can't predict what violence she might do. She opens the browser on her smart and finally checks the card in her hand, groaning when she sees the shop name.

"Creeper," Rei mutters, but she pulls up the Peach John website anyway. Models in elaborate, lacy bras holoproject from her smart, dancing in front of her eyes.

It's normal to get presents and gift cards from fans, especially the ones who know how little money she actually makes, but these ones make her skin crawl: the people who send her gift cards for places like Peach John and Bradelis NEO hoping that they can pay for her underwear, getting off on the thought that something they bought is holding her so intimately.

She navigates to the Home Goods section instead, picks out vases and scented candles and a complicated wire lamp. Whenever it arrives she'll take a selfy with the haul and post it to all her social scrolls, just to show her fans that there are some things she won't do. Little defiances like this are not victories but Rei feels obscurely like she has refused to give up some contested meter of turf.

▶

KOSAKA OPENS THE smart blinds on her windows remotely, waking Rei with a deliberate faceful of sunshine.

He can control any of her smart appliances remotely; signing over the access keys was a required contract clause for Hiyoko PRO idols. Kosaka had even gotten the company to pony up for a few other extras for her: a showerhead that lets him blast her with cold water when she dawdles and an alarm clock mounted purposefully on the far wall to force her out of bed.

There are no cameras, but for how well Rei's monitored there might as well be. Kosaka knows how long and deeply she sleeps by the sensors in her futon, the duration and temperature of her showers, and everything that goes in or out of the fridge. They've gotten into remote thermostat wars at least four times in the last year. Rei likes to keep the climate control unit set to 23 degrees but Kosaka is terrified that she'll catch a cold and risk her voice.

And of course, she hasn't had a friend over since V²
split up.

Getting up and going to work is, at this point, the
path of least resistance. Kosaka will continue to digitally
badger her until she does and trying to wait him out
has never worked in her favor. She's not sure why he
mostly left her to her own devices the prior two days. She
speculates that she rattled him at the handshake event. A
year ago, she'd have stayed in that stockroom to comfort
him and made her fans wait.

Rei grits her teeth, reminds herself that she has only
herself to blame for this, and starts the arduous checklist
that gets her out the door. Shower, skincare, clothing,
circle lenses, hair, purse, smart, mask, keys—it feels like
every step shaves a year off her life.

But when she checks her smart, Kosaka has pinged her
to let her know a self-driving taxi is on the way to take her
to the studio, and something in her blinks back to life.

It'd been nagging at the back of her mind for days: when
would she get to record the new single? She's supposed
to debut it at her next concert, and she's had the demo
track for "Hybrid Heart" for two weeks, even if she hasn't
listened to it since she put herself in Depression Timeout.

She knows it well enough to record it today, and to
know how she wants to change it.

It won't be easy. Kosaka never makes things easy. But if
she's lucky, he'll be so relieved to have her back in action
that she'll wrest a little control away from him, win a few
points. She'll ask for extra and let him bargain her down
so that she still gets the changes she wants most.

The recording studio Hiyoko PRO uses is located in
Ginza. Beholden to routine, she takes a selfy at the sign
by the door to post after she leaves. It's an older building,
but the equipment is top-quality, and Rei loves the warm
glow of the wood-paneled room. It's what she imagines the

inside of a beehive feels like: dim and amber-gold and full of a soothing hum.

Kosaka's beaten her there, but that's to be expected. He would never let her talk to anyone unsupervised and he'll arrive as early as necessary to make sure of it. He doesn't even leave her alone with costume fitters; he just waits behind a tall screen to give her a semblance of privacy.

"You look tired," he says. "Stayed up too late watching LYRICO videos again?"

She had, but that was on her personal account, and he shouldn't have access to a bioapp she installed independently. He might be bluffing, but what if he's not? She can't risk getting caught in a lie. So she laughs and pretends to think he's teasing her, and lets him set her up at the microphone.

She knows better than to tell him what she wants. Once she's in the booth, she sings the track straight through. Her first take is exactly as it's written, but she puts nothing into it—no interest, no charm, no energy. She lets it fall as flat as it feels to her, and when she's done she is grimly satisfied by Kosaka in the control room signaling her to take it from the top.

Her second take glows. She closes her eyes, sinks into that sensation of being safe and alone in her honey-colored cell, and flips the tentative little song from asking whether she is liked to demanding whether she is heard. She spins out the distance between herself and this hypothetical object of her affection, turning the boy in arm's reach into someone faraway and abstracted. She promises that she might learn to like this world, if she only knew that her song was echoing through it, and if you were only humming along somewhere, and if she could only spark a fever in you.

She thinks of Ririko, imagines Ririko hearing this song streaming somewhere, hearing it and knowing that Rei is reaching for her, full of love and remorse.

Rei is soaring through the bridge when Kosaka throws the door open.

"What is this?" he asks. She removes her headphones; he repeats himself.

Rei takes a deep breath. Technically, she has already done the reckless thing, but she still has a chance to apologize and walk it back. Instead, she plunges forward, secretly marveling at her own audacity. "I wanted to show you it could be better."

"It was fine the way it is."

"It was boring." But that's not the word she's looking for, so she tries again. "I mean, it felt small. Trivial. It doesn't have any—anything true in it."

"What do you mean, true?"

"Something that—"

"What do you *mean*?"

"I'm trying to say it, let me finish! Something that's important, you know? Something that feels solid and real."

"It's real for someone, even if it's not you. Plenty of girls feel this way."

"How would I know?" Rei asks. "My contract says I can't have relationships."

Kosaka's face shutters. "It doesn't need to have anything true in it. It just needs to get stuck in people's heads."

"But I can—"

"If you don't want to do your job, you can go back to your parents in Gunma. Maybe they'll pay for you to go back to college. Don't forget, Rei." Kosaka steps closer to her, well and truly inside the tiny bubble of personal space she is allotted by the world. He is a full twenty centimeters taller than her, and he allows her ample time to notice that before he continues. "There are plenty of other girls who want to be idols. You should be grateful I picked you."

She has badly misjudged his mood, Rei realizes. He has

never escalated this abruptly before, this viciously. She has to deescalate. She returns the headphones to their hook on the wall and approaches him, empty hands held out.

"I'm sorry," she says. "You're right. I was being selfish. It was silly of me." She holds her breath, waiting to see if she will have to grovel further.

But Kosaka has scooped her hands into his. "Our industry is in a precarious place right now," he says. "People don't care as much about fully human performances anymore. You're competing against computers—people mashing together clips out of a sound bank because they can't do anything but compose, or voices hiding behind avatars like LYRICO because they're not brave enough to be seen in public. If you don't want to lose to some shut-in NEET making dolls in their bedroom, you have to be as appealing as possible. You understand that, right?"

"I understand," Rei says, turning wide, guileless eyes on him, hoping that the lecture is done. He releases her hands and pats her on the head.

She records the song as it was written.

RIRIKO STEPPED BACK from the bidirectional mic between them and sighed. "When do you think we'll be done?" she whispered. "We've been here nearly six hours."

"When Mr. Kosaka decides we're done, I guess." Rei twisted a curl around her finger, darting a glance up at the control room. Kosaka, ensconced behind the glass, was deep in conversation with the producer and sound engineer. "Did you think I was sharp on that last take? I think I got sort of pitchy at the end of the hook."

Ririko shrugged, the motion displacing her bangs. She reached up to brush them back from her eyes. "You sounded fine to me."

"You sounded really good on the A-melo," Rei offered. "It'll be fun when we get to do this live!"

"Yeah," Ririko said, but Rei could tell her heart wasn't in it at all. There were no chairs in the room; Ririko sat down on the floor, knees pulled up to her chest. Rei joined her immediately.

"Are you okay?"

"I'm...I'm just tired," Ririko said. "That taping for Yoruyan took all day yesterday, and I didn't count on being here so long. There was something else I wanted to do today..." She pressed her lips shut, her eyes clouded.

Rei hadn't moved, but she felt a lurch as though she'd reached the end of the escalator before she was ready to walk.

"It's nothing," Ririko said finally, perhaps unsettled by Rei's watchful silence. "Don't worry about me.Hey, listen to this. I made it up last night."

Ririko's smart was dressed in a case that looked like a chocolate bar, neat grid lines molded onto it. She hadn't changed her lockscreen since high school; it still showed the 2.5D avatars Rei had designed for them in Avidance, perfectly posed. Rei leaned in so that Ririko could tuck her earbuds into Rei's ears with deft fingers that smelled faintly of hand sanitizer.

A stuttering rhythm filled Rei's senses: Ririko's hands clapping, laying down a simple beat. Her voice was soft on the recording—she must have been trying not to bother the neighbors—but her song was tender and insistent, demanding response. Rei thought of a nature documentary she'd seen on NHK a long time ago. The wolves howled at the night the way Ririko did now: the world is so cold that her bones feel empty, her heart rattling in the hollow void of her ribcage, and the city neon has drowned out the stars—but you're here too, in the cold and the fog, and somehow we can dance through it together, can't we?

The snippet was over too soon, and Rei didn't realize until it ended that she'd closed her eyes. When she opened them again, the warm honey lights of the recording studio left her dazzled and blinded.

"What...do you think?" Ririko asked when Rei pulled out the earbuds.

"It's good," Rei whispered. "It's really good. Have you shown Mr. Kosaka?"

"Not yet. Should I?"

"Of course! He'll love it too. And then we can record it for real!"

There was no static, but both girls heard the second the loudspeaker was activated. The air in the room tasted different. "Let's have another take," Kosaka said from the control booth. "Rei, careful on the hook. You're going just a little high."

Rei glanced at Ririko ruefully—*told you so*—and turned to face the window, raising her voice and stepping closer to her microphone. "Mr. Kosaka, Ririko's not feeling well. Can she go home? I'll stay and finish up."

"Rei!" Ririko whispered, but the note of relief in her voice was unmistakable.

"We need vocals from both of you," he said.

"Will it cost a lot more if we record separately?" Rei asked. "I mean, the instrumental is prerecorded anyway. She really, seriously feels ill, Mr. Kosaka."

"Ririko?" he asked.

"I—I can stay," Ririko said softly. "I just have a really bad headache. It's so loud in here." She closed her eyes. Rei was always silently impressed by Ririko's acting. Ririko had gotten out of class any number of times in high school with a skillfully feigned headache. Her trick was to pretend she was determined to power through it, which generally convinced authority figures that she was a step from collapse. Rei had never mastered the art herself.

Ririko forced her large, limpid eyes open, turning them towards the control booth. She looked as though even that movement pained her.

Rei heard Kosaka's surrender in the quality of his pause, and at last he said, "I'm calling you a taxi, Ririko. We'll book time to finish your side of the vocals later this week."

When Ririko hugged Rei goodbye, fever-hot through their matching chiffon blouses, she whispered her thanks into the dainty shell of Rei's ear. Rei wouldn't know for weeks that she'd stolen her friend not a day of sleep behind drawn curtains, but an afternoon with her secret boyfriend. All she knew at the time was that Ririko came back to the office the next day smiling and ready to sing.

She'd dabbed concealer under Ririko's eyes and they showed Kosaka the new song, crowding around his desk to play the recording off Ririko's smart. He hated it, hated that Ririko had created something without his permission or oversight.

He'd been gentle about it. Sternness and scolding weren't a part of their relationship in those days. He'd even tried to smile as he reminded them to leave these things to the professionals, but his pursed lips quelled them in a way that direct criticism never could. Rei had thought it wasn't worth disappointing or irritating him. Kosaka had been in this business for years; he knew best, and she wasn't ready to risk losing his mentorship.

SHE **WONDERS IF** Kosaka will bring it up, when she sees him the next day; whether, now that she's had her scolding, further punishment may yet be in store. Will it be the silent treatment, maybe? Or will he threaten to hurt himself, forcing her to talk him down and comfort him? Will she have to perch next to his chair, drying his tears and rubbing his back in a locked meeting room again?

Rei considers, not for the first time, moving to a different production agency. It's a fantasy, really. After fourteen months as a solo artist she's both too big and not big enough to do that. If her first single had sold poorly and she'd been dropped, maybe she could have convinced another company to give her a second chance. A virtual agency would probably have been willing to put her behind an avatar and set her up to stream. If she shut her mouth and smiled, she'd do well as a gravure model. Or if she was already the superstar Kosaka promised to make her, and there was a chance she could take her fans with her, she might be able to sign with someone new on the strength of her past sales. But she is caught in the awful middle, and she has seen too many other idols fall from this position. Even if she could fight the contract clauses designed to keep her at Hiyoko PRO, who would take her in? Rei would be called disloyal, hard to work with, someone who'd turned her back on the company that invested in her training. No one would want her. She'd blackball herself without Kosaka or the CEO having to make a single call.

And if they did decide to retaliate, she'd be helpless. Hiyoko PRO has an entire stable of idols and actors more famous and more desired than Rei. If Hiyoko PRO sent out the ultimatum, denied any program featuring Rei access to its other talents...well, then it just makes economic sense to freeze Rei out.

But when she reaches the office, Kosaka is making a studied effort to pretend that they never disagreed at all. He greets her with casual warmth and Rei's relief temporarily knocks all other cognitive function offline, which is why she almost fails to notice the young girl on the visitor couch across from Kosaka's desk.

She's clutching a red tote bag in her lap and wearing a tissue-weight pink sweater and jeans, but her knees are pulled together tightly as if she's wearing a school uniform. Her hair is jet black and bluntly princess-cut, falling to her elbows, thick fringe obscuring her forehead. Rei suspects that hair has never been plasma-permed or dyed.

The girl stares up at her, apparently too awestruck to speak.

Rei bows slightly. "Nice to meet you. I'm Yoshizawa Rei. What's your name?"

"It's really you! I like your music," the girl blurts in one breath and flushes pink. "I mean—"

"That's Aimi," Kosaka cuts in. "She's new here. I'll be managing her from now on."

At her look he says, "Surely you didn't think you'd always be my only idol. When Yukarin was active I managed two other groups besides her." Those groups and his private

office upstairs had been taken away from him when
Yukarin abruptly retired from the industry, but Rei knows
better than to point that out. She's been Kosaka's only
assignment for as long as she's known him, first as half of
Venus Versus and then as a solo act. If he has clearance to
take on a new idol, his success with her must have finally
redeemed him in the eyes of the higher-ups.

She should be pleased for him. This is what he's been
working towards for over three years. But he doesn't need
to elaborate for Rei to register the threat: here is someone
younger and prettier and more pliable than you. Will you
obey or be usurped?

"I'm Araki Aimi," the girl finally manages to say. "I
know I have a lot to learn, but I'm going to do my best!"

"Oh, I guess I'm your senior, aren't I?" Rei laughs and
plops down on the other end of the couch. There were
one or two younger girls in high school who had thought
she was pretty, but no one ever really looked to her for
mentoring. She hadn't joined the student council or any
club activities that would have given her the chance. "Let
me know if I can help you with anything. Welcome to
Hiyoko PRO."

Her mind is whirring. With two of them to manage,
Kosaka will have to finally relax his grip. He can't be in
two places at once. He'll have to trust her to go to lessons
and rehearsals alone at the very least.

"So what are today's plans?" Rei asks, turning to watch
Kosaka swipe and jab at his smart. But Aimi speaks first.

"I'm going to voice lessons with you," she says. "It was
in the schedule Mr. Kosaka emailed me last night."

Merely splitting Kosaka's attention with another idol
isn't enough to make Rei jealous, but this sends a wave of
hot indignation roaring up her body. Once upon a time
she'd looked forward to that midnight email laying out
the next day's schedule. Those emails stopped the day
Ririko left V^2. Rei has been trying to earn that trust back

for more than a year—when she's not even the one who broke the rules!—but Aimi has just been given it? The unfairness makes her teeth hurt.

She hides it under a smile. "Great! Have you taken voice lessons before? Don't worry if you haven't. Mai, my trainer, is really nice."

"I haven't had lessons, but I'm in the light music club at school."

Rei clocks the present tense and turns to look the other girl full in the face. "How old are you?"

"Sixteen." The word comes out a little hesitant, as if Aimi expects to be mocked for it.

"Oh, wow!" Rei exclaims, always quick to soothe. "That's impressive, getting scouted so young! And you're not quitting school early? How amazing. I could never!"

The effusive praise seems to set Aimi at ease. Her shoulders come down from around her ears. "I'd rather be an idol full time, but my parents won't let me. They said I should at least finish high school. Mr. Kosaka is even hiring a tutor to help me keep my grades up."

"That's good." Rei leans in conspiratorially. "I dropped out of college to be an idol. My parents are still so mad that they won't even talk to me." Her parents trade water futures on the virtual exchange. To them, idols are physical laborers. Sometimes, when she's rubbing a sore muscle, Rei thinks they aren't entirely wrong.

Aimi's eyes go wide as a startled laugh jumps from her throat. "I—oh, that's awful, I'm sorry for laughing—"

"Don't apologize. I don't mind it," Rei says, and hopes the girl is too naive to pick up on her bravado. "I'd rather be an idol than anything else."

That much, at least, isn't a lie.

Now that she's relaxed a bit, Aimi keeps chatting while Kosaka shepherds them into a company car and drives them to their music school. Rei learns that Aimi has lived in Tokyo her whole life. She's always wanted to be an

idol, but her parents didn't think it was a feasible career
path so they refused to invest in singing or dance lessons.
Eventually they promised that if Aimi passed auditions at
an agency they'd let her become an idol. She started going
to tryouts when she was fourteen, on any day she didn't
have to be at school. She went to Rei's live at Diver City
six months ago, and that's why she went to Hiyoko PRO's
open audition recently—

"Really?" Rei asks. She can't help but be flattered.
"Because of me?"

"*Thanks* to you," Aimi bubbles. She grins, and suddenly
breaks into one of Rei's songs. "*No matter where or when,
my heart's flying to you, so wait up!*"

Rei catches Kosaka's eye in the rearview mirror. "Isn't
it nice to be young?" she jokes, mimicking the tone he uses
to tease her. He laughs, and despite all her resentment she
feels a spark of pride.

By the time they pull up to the school Rei has almost
convinced herself that having Aimi around will be fun,
like getting the little sister she always wished for. Ririko's
presence, through school and beyond, had always been
her buffer against only-child angst. This optimism
withstands even Mai's failure to question the inclusion of a
newcomer, revealing that Rei was truly the last to be told
about Aimi. It carries her through lip rolls and scales and
the usual battery of warmups.

It falls apart when Mai asks them to harmonize.

Mai still has some old V^2 sheet music stuffed in the
back of Rei's carte, and Aimi says she knows "A Hello at
the End of the World," so fine, why not try it? Rei agrees
with a smile even though some tiny scrap of loyalty or love
kicks inside her.

They trade lines through the A-melo, Aimi singing
Ririko's part and Rei pretending not to mind it, and their
voices blend in unison for the B-melo. Rei's whole body
tightens up. She's drowning in the melody filling their

little soundproofed lesson room. Her vision shimmers. If
she leaned against one of the foam-padded walls to steady
herself, she might sink in and fall forever.

It has been so long since these words were in her mouth
but she remembers every one of them. She remembers love.

The refrain jars her, drags her gasping back onto shore.
Their voices are still ringing in unison, and they shouldn't
be, and the song feels like it's collapsing in on itself. It
takes a full measure for Rei to understand why.

Aimi has switched parts. She's singing Rei's high
melody line. She doesn't know, or won't try, Ririko's
lower harmony: more work for less glory, but absolutely
necessary for the song to sound right.

Rei glances at Mai for help. The teacher's eyes flick
back and forth between Rei and the sheet music, but she
keeps playing.

Rei switches onto the harmony mid-phrase. She's heard
it hundreds of times, but now she has to think about the
notes, actively fighting her own muscle memory. She
should be supporting Aimi's melody, but when Aimi's
voice soars on the long E5 at the end of the chorus Rei
wants to join her up there. She's scraping the bottom of
her range, unused to these lower notes.

How had Ririko ever managed to shut out Rei's melody
line and stick so firmly to her lower harmony, never
wavering? How had she been so sure that she was in tune
when they were singing different notes entirely? All Rei
wants to do is sing the notes she knows by heart, her part,
in unison with Aimi. It is not the shape of the song she
shared with Ririko. She'd like to leave that one locked safe
in her memory.

And yet, at the end of the song, Mai gives Rei an
approving nod. "A little sharp, but you're not used to
singing that part, so it's to be expected. You did well
enough for being surprised."

Her words don't meet Rei's threshold for praise. She

wants to do well, not well enough; to be good without concessions or qualifiers muddying her achievement. She smiles anyway because she is supposed to, and the lesson ticks onward.

But she can't get Aimi's lovely pure E5 out of her head. That part of the melody had always been Rei's private property, but now...young and pretty and obedient, with a mouth full of Rei's songs...

Rei is scared. She should be scared, because she is replaceable.

▶

WHEN THEY RETURN to the office Kosaka packs Rei off to one of the dance studios upstairs for rehearsal.

"Don't be a bother to the techs," he says. "I'm taking Aimi around to a couple of TV stations for introductions, but I'll be back before your stream starts."

Rei has scarcely an hour for rest and dinner and costuming between the final run-through and the real thing, but she is lucky to have even this. Some days her last rehearsal runs late and she has to rush through hair and makeup to be ready when the stream starts. A lot of idols are uncomfortable with streaming lives; bothered by the silence of the audience, mainly. Rei's not one of them. Screaming into the void holds no fear for her. If anything, it's a comfort.

She stares down a vitamin jelly pack and wishes for almost anything else: a cheeseburger with pineapple, a sizzling grill full of kalbi and jō-mino, all things that would make her calorie meter sound the alarm. But she's not allowed so much as half an egg salad sandwich until the show's over. Kosaka terrified her once, years ago—her and Ririko both—with the story of Yukarin sprinting offstage at her first concert after only three songs to throw up the onigiri she'd eaten before showtime, bloated and sick from dancing on a full stomach.

Rei holds each mouthful of artificially sweetened blueberry jelly in her mouth until it is warm and swallows slowly, a little at a time, to prevent hiccups. She's never had a real blueberry—too hard to find and too expensive besides—but she hopes this isn't what they taste like, because that would be awfully disappointing. She lets a glucose tab dissolve on her tongue for a boost of energy. She wants a glass of water or three but she can't risk how it might distend her belly. Besides, Rei won't be able to excuse herself to the bathroom during the stream. She'll wait until she's on air and reward herself with cool, measured sips between songs. It'll taste sweeter if she earns it, anyway.

The streaming lives are always short; she'll do a five-song set, take a couple audience questions carefully pre-screened by Kosaka, and remind her fans what time *Entropy Fighter Mizuki* airs, as if they're ever given a chance to forget. Kosaka posts reminders on her social scrolls sixty and then fifteen minutes before new episodes premiere.

The whole thing will take a bit less than an hour. Hiyoko PRO has done extensive testing and analysis: after about the forty-minute mark, audience interest starts to flag. The viewers open other tabs and leave their idols running in the background, smiling for people too stingy to look at them, and then they close the window once they want to listen to something else they've come across in the interminable scrolls of their socmed accounts, kicking off a snowball effect of viewer attrition. Rei hates watching her numbers drop when she loses their attention. It feels like falling.

Rei slurps the last drops of blueberry sludge from her foil pouch and thwangs it into the noncombustibles bin. She'll pull good numbers tonight, she promises herself, ignoring how little control she really has over that. She'll keep their eyes on her, she'll steal every speck of the attention that makes her an idol. It is not real love, and it is what she wants. Rei has trained herself to think "and" instead of "but," erasing the concessive from the idea.

She wrestles her costume on by herself. Kosaka never bothers reserving a dresser for streams, since Rei doesn't mess around with quick changes between songs. The short, spangled skirt is a mosaic of a thousand skies and oceans, blues stormy and heavenly competing for space, chasing each other across the digiprint. This moving pattern is still in the dev phase. Streams under controlled studio conditions are a more forgiving trial ground than "out" shows. The white button-down she tucks into the waistband briefly turns her into a sci-fi parody of a schoolgirl, but the coat pulls it all together.

The sleeveless duster's hem falls all the way to her knees in a wave of night-sky navy. Every time Rei spins the whole coat shines with a thousand tiny diamond points of light, the built-in accelerometer briefly blessing her with stars she hasn't seen since she moved to Tokyo.

She thinks less about Gunma than she'd expected she would, after she moved to the city. She and Ririko had applied to all the same schools, enrolled together so they could move into the same student housing complex. By the end of summer they were barely even going to class, spending as much time as possible at auditions. They'd been planning it since high school, practicing their dance moves behind the gymnasium or up on the roof at lunch. Neither of them, despite what they'd told their parents about their chosen majors and the internships they'd apply for, ever intended to be anything but an idol.

Hiyoko PRO signed them before they had time to fail the term-end exams. It didn't stop Rei's parents from being furious over the money they'd wasted on tuition.

As a general rule, Rei does her own makeup. She's good at it; she's been practicing for years, after all. She always helped Ririko with her eyeliner back when they were Venus Versus. Now that Ririko has been left behind with the dust of her past and Rei doesn't have a friend to put her hair up, Kosaka hires hairstylists off the company's list of affiliate salons. Never the same person twice; he won't risk Rei getting to know people, making friends. Rei has grown used to stilted small talk with strangers as part of her pre-show routine. It makes the moment she steps onstage that much more freeing: the safety of indirect interaction, chatting to people who can only respond en masse. It doesn't matter what she says. No matter how banal, the response will be an indistinct roar. She likes it better this way. No need to struggle for a relevant, coherent reply. Interaction without pressure.

When her last curl is set, refreshed with the cold-iron, and her lips perfectly spackled with gloss, she opens the door into the streaming studio.

They told her once that the room had been originally used for dance practice. It'd been converted during the streaming boom a few decades before Rei was born, and periodic upgrades kept it up to modern standards. Kosaka, in discussion with the tech team, barely spares her a glance as he waves her into position. The lighting tech begins calibrating the variable plasma lights, casting a rosy glow onto Rei. She shivers a little under the lights. Variable plasma throws off a cooling effect— ideal to keep her from sweating, but less pleasant when she stands still.

A stream never goes live precisely on time; too many people miss the start, when that's the case. Kosaka counts Rei in at ten past the hour.

And then the screens mounted on the wall—clock, chat display, set list, viewer count—light up. A giddy relief floods Rei's bones, all-consuming gratitude steadying her with its gentle hand. The tally shows that her audience has already broken four digits. Rei wonders if Aimi, safely returned to her parents' house, is one of them.

They still love her today. They must, because here
they are. They've shown up for her. It's the only way she
knows for sure—because while some people tell her they're
unfollowing her, the vast majority will simply stop tuning in.

She reaches back for them, her voice and body
brimming with everything she wants to make them
feel tonight. It would be nice, she thinks, if her feelings
reached them.

She glides from MC segments into songs and back
with practiced ease, and doesn't even mind the lack of
applause. The chat screen is moving too fast for her eyes
to track, flooded with messages and lines of 8888s to
represent clapping. All her dopamine clusters are glowing:
A8, A9, A10 and onward, lighting her up. She can't look
at the scroll too long without getting dizzy. She wishes she
could tell Kosaka to turn on the notification sounds and
feed them straight into her earpiece, every ping setting off
a popping party of serotonin fireworks. This sort of vague
wave of response, its actual content indistinguishable, is
safe, cathartic, in a way direct engagement can never be.
This performance is a declaration, not a conversation.

And Rei knows how eloquently she does it. She has
never been convinced that she has any fundamental
goodness, but this is the closest she comes: when she is
spinning, darting, smiling across a studio or a stage, when
her voice is raised in song, when she knows everything she
is made of and is at peace with it all.

The fourth song ends, and Kosaka's voice is low and
steady in her ear. "Good job on that key change. Tighten
up your posture; you'll look less bloated if you stop
slouching. What did you eat for dinner, anyway?"

Rei keeps smiling for the camera through her fury.
She can't answer him, and he knows by now that she
doesn't eat dinner until after she's done performing.
He's just—just making sure she's still on her game, still
paying attention, not getting lost in her own hype. But he

has forced her to remember her body, brought her back into it again. Her soul, which had felt so expansive, so transcendent, contracts. It nestles back into hiding under her diaphragm. It will not come out again tonight.

She is a professional. She keeps dancing regardless, spine straightened and shoulders tightened, delivering what Kosaka has deemed her most appealing angles to the audience.

▶

SHE FEELS HOLLOW when she gets home. Her soul keeps shrinking until Rei can't even feel it anymore, can't find it, a tiny shard of glitter lost under the dustheap of her self.

Sometimes it feels this way, when the lights are off and the costumes and makeup put away. She comes down from the dopamine high, as if the blood has been flushed from her veins and replaced by saline, and she just feels empty.

There's nothing to be done for it, really. She'd like a lemon ice—for some reason it's awfully hard to remember that she's sad when lemon is dancing bright acid over her tongue—but she hasn't got it in her to go out again to buy one, and it'd put her over her calorie ceiling for the day anyway. She might as well go to bed. Scrubbed, soaked, her skin still flushed from the bath, she rolls out her futon, crawls in, and does not sleep.

Rei stares up into the dark, and does not sleep.

She carefully presses the fingertips of one hand over the edge of her opposite palm, tapping and massaging her way down the lung meridian, and does not sleep.

How many more years might it take before Kosaka can't touch her mood anymore? Before he can't make her feel unremarkable, unpretty, unlovable, worthless? It only takes a few words to remind her how fragile everything she's achieved really is. It would be so horribly easy for her fans to stop loving her.

The music is her only real shield from anything, and
even that isn't perfect. On days she hits every note easily,
days when her vibrato trembles sweet in her throat
until all her muscles loosen, she is at ease. If she can't
quite find the rhythm, if her voice is even a little pitchy,
the shame of her own fallibility turns her anxious and
tearful.

They love her voice, her face, her body. Rei does not
make the mistake of believing that they love *her*. All
these things they love must be presented perfectly if
she is to continue being adored. A cracked high note,
a pimple, a badly tailored costume or a kilo too much
weight could cost her everything. After all, her ridiculous,
awful, disobedient body cannot deliver the consistent
performance of a digital doll and its sound bank. It can't
even manage the reassuring sameness of the avatars that
better singers than her hide behind.

LYRICO, she thinks, is lucky not to be a whole person.
LYRICO has never given an interview—never made a
sound that wasn't music. She has no interiority to offer up
on the altar in exchange for adoration. If all she has to
offer is skill, that is all she can be loved for.

Rei reaches in and up with her mind, looking for her
server uplink, and snags on NeuroDouga like a hangnail
on silk. She tells herself that she intends to load up
some quiet piano, maybe a seaside atmosphere to lull
her to sleep, but her impulses outpace her thoughts and
LYRICO claims a corner of her mind for a stage, singing
and dancing with unflagging energy.

When the app was new, it had felt intrusive to have
someone else performing in her head, but she's gotten used
to it. It's more or less like letting music play in another
browser tab. Now the only streams she finds intrusive are
her own. She can't help watching herself, scrutinizing
every moment of her performance and cataloging every
imperfection.

She doesn't need to load up the archive footage to know that she did poorly on that last number tonight. She let Kosaka rattle her and she finished weak. Another night like this and *they won't love you anymore* just might become a self-fulfilling prophecy. What would be worse, to go out in a blaze of bad press like Ririko did or to fade out into owakon obscurity?

At least Ririko's scandal had left some scars to remember her by.

With sudden and awful clarity, Rei wants a drink. There's an unopened can of Yebisu in the back of her fridge, bought in a fit of rebellion and never drunk. But if more alcohol than a sip of mouthwash crosses her lips while she is away from Kosaka, her bioapps will ping him a notification, and he'll call to scold her about empty calories and bloating and what a PR nightmare an addiction would cause. It's just not worth the lecture.

She tries to drown out her thoughts by humming along to the song in her head. At some point the autoqueue and its algorithm moved on without her paying attention, and she is listening to a Venus Versus song now.

On another night she would critique her younger self: how tentatively she moved, how she was too afraid to reach for notes at either end of her comfort zone. She'd reflect on how immature she was, relying on Ririko's voice to prop up her own. Or she'd shut it off, unable to bear the embarrassment of ever letting anyone see her give such an unpolished performance. She'd dodge her guilt. She'd do anything to avoid looking full-on at Ririko, the ashes she'd risen from to become an ideal, idealized phoenix of an idol.

Ririko deserves better than to be ashes. Tonight, in her hollowness, Rei has enough space inside her to acknowledge that.

So she watches the PV playing on the inside of her forehead, and she tries to find some affection for these two figures out of the past. They're singing "A Hello at the End of the World," and while Rei doesn't quite look at the camera straight on, she smiles every time her eyes meet Ririko's.

And here is something that small, innocent Rei shares with the one watching her: she too is soaring untouchable and invincible on a current made of music, her joy apparent as her voice swells in the chorus, her high notes supported by Ririko's unshakable harmony. *"It's okay if it doesn't reach you; I'll still sing it anyway, because it's proof I was here."*

They hadn't known, when they filmed this, that it would be the last song they released together.

Rei—not the Rei of memory, but the present Rei— blinks back horrible hot tears. She twists at the inside of her mind to kill the bioapp, dismisses the shudder of the little prompt that asks permission to report the force-close to the manufacturer.

She retrieves her smart from the nightstand to dose herself with the parts of the internet she won't let into her body. The social scrolls are fairly quiet at this hour that is both very late night and very early morning. She mainly follows other idols, who are sleeping now, or at least smart enough to pretend so.

Before she thinks better of it she has found V²'s old Sunny Labo commercial, where the camera cuts between Venus Versus making themselves up backstage with the summer limited palette and dancing together under the spotlights of O-EAST as "OVER HORIZON" plays. Two summers ago that advertisement had been ubiquitous. She'd seen it rolling silent on the train, heard it playing in drugstores, watched their fans post dance covers on NeuroDouga. The whole world had turned magical, a hall of mirrors where Ririko and Rei smiled up at screens full of themselves and understood themselves to be loved.

"This is still my favorite song," she swipes into her smart, and stops.

If she posts, how many people will tell her they liked her better with Ririko next to her?

If she posts, how quickly will Kosaka catch on and take it down? He has her credentials; he can log in and delete it without a word to her. And how will he punish her for it? Will he shift all his attentions, all his efforts, onto Aimi? After all, she can't fully believe Aimi isn't meant to replace her.

Rei takes a deep breath, counts to three, and decides to throw her heart into the void. As soon as the post is out there, bracketed by ads for the 109 summer collections and a jewelry subscription box, she backs out of the app to ward off the immediate impulse to delete it.

Even if she deleted it right now, she tells herself, Kosaka will have seen a screenshot by morning. She can't take this one back.

It feels better than she expected.

THE WORST PART of the scandal should have been the way she was suddenly and abruptly severed from Ririko. Later, it would be.

But at first, the worst part was that everyone kept tagging her when they posted about it.

Kosaka called her as soon as her bioapps indicated even a hazy consciousness.

"Reply to no one," he ordered. "Don't say or write a single word that I haven't cleared first."

By the time Rei looked at her smart's homescreen she was grateful for the directive. Her unread notifications had climbed to triple digits before she even woke up that awful morning. She took a screenshot, texted Kosaka a draft to get permission, and posted it to her scroll with the caption: "I'm sorry, but there's no way I can reply to

everyone individually!" and hoped that might buy her
some grace.

It did, barely. It bought her the time to get to the office
and find Kosaka three beers in at barely 9:00, attempting
to drown himself in a bathroom sink.

"This was supposed to be my comeback. I can't take
another scandal," he sobbed when Rei yanked him out
of the water, scraping his skull against the faucet in her
panic. Abruptly she remembered how the universally
beloved Yukarin's career had ended: with an early-
morning arrest, after she'd drunkenly struck a pedestrian
with her vintage Skyline.

She'd always wondered if that was why Kosaka kept her
on such a short leash.

"You can't take another," she said, "and I can't take one
at all. But it's not fair to throw me away over something I
didn't even know about!"

"You should have known. She's your best friend."

"Clearly the feeling wasn't mutual." The bitterness in
her voice, ringing off the bathroom tiles, shocked Rei. "I
know I'm not as good a singer as Ririko. But I can be a
better idol."

Kosaka stooped to let Rei wipe his face with the
rough paper towels from the packet on the counter as
he considered this. He hadn't noticed yet that he was
bleeding onto his collar from the faucet wound and Rei
had no idea how to broach the topic, so she dabbed at the
bright little stain with a damp towel as best she could.

In the time it took to clean his face and his glasses,
she had ample time to consider the various precipices
on which she perched. He could throw her away right
now—because Venus Versus needed both of them to be
worthwhile, because she should have kept Ririko in line.
She was inviting scandal on herself just by being alone in
this bathroom with Kosaka. If that one got out there'd be
no salvaging either of their reputations.

He seemed to notice this last too, frowning.

"Go make some coffee," he said. Kosaka wrung water out of his necktie and shot his cuffs. "Wait at my desk. I'm going to talk to the president." There was steel in his voice. Rei was thankful for it.

What he said to the president that morning, what promises he made—these were more items on the list of things he didn't tell her. "Leave the business to me," he said. "All you have to do is sing, dance, and look pretty."

At the time, it was a relief to be told that. These were the things she was best at; she'd practiced them for years. She could put herself into Kosaka's hands, let him drive her career, sink into the mindless and downy comfort of letting someone else take over. If there was any reason not to obey him, she didn't, couldn't see it back then.

肆

KOSAKA DEACTIVATES HER smart's silent mode a full hour before her alarms should wake her. Dazed, Rei doesn't answer his call.

A moment later his voice blares from the autolock intercom on the wall, the one she only uses to buzz the postman up when she's ordered something too big for the mailbox. She's suspected he had access to it for months, and now she finally has confirmation.

"What have you done?" His angry voice fuzzes and crackles in the speaker. If she picks up the handset, would she be able to talk back? "I'm sending you a link. I want you to watch it right away."

Oh no, it's an entertainment news show, isn't it? Things have been slow lately. This could just barely qualify as news. But the link, when Rei opens it on her smart, takes her to a video on the dryware version of NeuroDouga.

It's clear that AventureP, whoever they are, has prioritized speed over quality. LYRICO doesn't dance. She stands on a small round stage planted in the middle of a black screen, wearing a simple white sundress, and sings the most stripped-down version of "OVER HORIZON" imaginable. It's just LYRICO's voice—her producer's voice, using the doll as a mask—and a single piano. It's lovelier than Rei could dream.

Even something this simple would have taken hours to make. The hem of LYRICO's dress flutters when she moves. Her hair slides over her shoulders when she bows her head. If this is some kind of response to Rei's post, AventureP must have been up all night, syncing the movements of LYRICO's mouth to her words. Rei checks the timestamp. The video has been live for less than an hour, and it has already broken a five-figure view count.

It is a gift to her. It cannot possibly be for her. She thinks about pareidolia, apophenia, those strange foreign loanwords she'd had to learn for entrance exams. Is that what she's doing, reading signs and omens where there are none? Has her sense of pattern recognition gone haywire?

She calls Kosaka back, because she knows she has to sometime. It'll be worse if she puts it off.

"What were you thinking?" he barks. She is ready for this.

"I thought it'd be humanizing," Rei said. "It's weird how we pretend the whole first two years of my career never happened. People notice that, like at the handover event last week. I thought I should do something that looked like it was all okay—to show there aren't any hard feelings about V², or whatever."

For an excuse she invented in under three minutes, it's passable. At first she even thinks he's bought it, but—

"Liar," Kosaka says. "But it's already out there, so we'll have to work around it."

It is a more measured response than she expected. But even that, when she considers it, makes sense. She's harder to control with tears or shouting at a distance. No sense wasting good drama when it won't produce his desired outcome.

"Get dressed and get to the studio," he orders. "I have a plan."

Rei winces, but at least for once the consequences are for something she did herself.

BY THE TIME she reaches the Hiyoko PRO office two hours later, well before she was even meant to be in today, the ripples her single post has caused have made themselves apparent.

Her original post has been reposted over six hundred times, nearly half of those with commentary, and "liked" over five thousand times.

"OVER HORIZON" is trending on her social scroll.

The original Venus Versus release of "OVER HORIZON" has shot up to #1 on the NeuroChoku download chart.

And Kosaka has installed a quarantine function on all her official social accounts, where he will now review all of Rei's posts before releasing them to the public, because clearly he can no longer trust her to behave responsibly. Even if Rei knew how to explain it, he would never understand that this could all have been avoided if he had trusted her more in the first place.

He paces the office like a caged thing, raking his hands through his black hair. His hair gel has shed flakes onto his shoulders. His tie sits askew. His eyes shine, threatening to spill over.

How much of it is a performance for her benefit? Just as she deploys Soft Café Nymphette to soothe him, perhaps Overwrought Guardian is a character he's invented to curb her disobedience. Certainly he can't storm or cry in front of the CEO. He wouldn't have a job if he did, so he must be able to control his behavior when necessary. She dislikes this train of thought immensely, but knows better than to dismiss it.

"We can't let LYRICO control this narrative," he says. "We need to make sure the focus is on you. Not that goddamn doll, not Venus Versus. You."

Well, at least he's not making it about Aimi. When will

he deploy her as his shiny new stick to bring Rei back in line? When will he push Rei out of the spotlight to make room for Aimi? Surely there isn't room for both of them.

Rei wonders, several hours too late, whether her post might stir up interest in Ririko again. Will some reporter decide that the world deserves to know where she is now?

Would that be a bad thing, really? Then Rei could know she was okay, at least. Maybe she'd even get to see her again, and Rei could apologize, and—

The crunk of Kosaka's Pacifix dispenser, like a bone in a meat grinder, brings her back to reality. Pacifix is his prescription of choice for its efficiency: it's autosynthesized from supplements mixed into each of Kosaka's meals and hoarded in his body against times of need. She watches the lines around his fretful mouth slacken as the drug flows through him. She is suddenly and keenly aware of how early it is: they have the floor to themselves, every desk empty at this hour. She is alone with him, and his physicality is enough to cow her: he's a gangly nerd, but he is still larger and stronger and angry at her. Rei resents how her shoulders curve forward, how her head droops on her slender neck as she hunches in on herself. She makes herself take up as little space as possible. His threat must be met with her frailty and harmlessness. It's the fastest way to end this confrontation: be small, be weak, give in.

Kosaka doesn't look directly at her, but he must catch her cowering in his peripheral vision, because he stops pacing. He stacks his vertebrae back up and shakes his head, putting himself back together.

He is always in control of her, but in this awful moment as he regains control of himself, Rei understands: he will never, ever let her see Ririko again. Not unless he orchestrated it, scripted it, oversaw the filming and editing. A documentary jewel in her crown; another experience he could suck all the joy out of.

It would be better to never see Ririko again than to let him ruin it.

"We need content," he says. "Lots of it. We'll upload so much Rei to the internet this week that the whole world will forget any other idols even exist."

When he puts it like that, a pang of naked want rings through her, and Rei's gut curdles with shame. She's so easily seduced. He spins, closes the distance between them as if he can smell her weakness.

"Do you trust me?" He raises a hand to cup her jaw as if he could compel the answer from her. Once upon a time, Rei would have leaned into the touch, believing wholly that he had her best interests at heart. Now she is only repulsed by the sweaty heat of his palm.

But: "Yes," she lies, gazing up at him and pretending not to mind his coffee breath at close range. "Of course I trust my manager."

"Put some more coffee on. I'm going to make some reservations."

If Rei needed a reminder of the weight behind the Hiyoko PRO name, of Kosaka's clout, here it is. He only has to ask, and the world opens like a flower in his hands. Camera operators, a chauffeured car, same-day access to a popular restaurant before business hours even start—all the things that other producers would have to arrange in advance—are easy for him to line up with a few words.

After she brings him his umpteenth coffee of the day, he sends her to the dressing room to prep. Half an hour later, as she is putting on her makeup, he joins her.

Today, Kosaka explains as Rei dabs and stipples and paints, they will batch content for later release on her NeuroDouga channel. Based on her previous statistics, the content her fans are most interested in are Q&As, makeup reviews, and gourmet experiences.

They always want to see such mundane things. The questions surprise her sometimes with how trivial they are: her favorite coffee at Family Mart, her usual ramen toppings, where she bought a certain pair of shoes. Rei has learned by now which things to lie about. She can be honest when she says what shampoo she uses or ranks her favorite onigiri fillings. She never reviews a restaurant unless she's resigned to never going there again for fear of being spotted, recognized, approached.

Makeup reviews are less artificial than her other performances, but somehow Rei doesn't mind it as she holds up products for the camera. She's willing to be generous with these tidbits. Everything about her appearance takes work, whether it's by her or a stylist, and she won't let that go unrecognized. So she presents eyeshadows and blushes to the camera, specifying which she uses onstage and which are for everyday wear, and digs through her mycopleather purse to show off her favorite lipstick, the one with peppermint oil in it.

Kosaka has chosen the restaurant for today's grand gourmet tour, a hole-in-the-wall ramen shop near the Nishi-Azabu intersection. Rei's fine with that; it means she won't have to pick something to give up. She's starting to run out of safe restaurants. She doesn't go out much to begin with, given how tight her budget is, and there are so few places she can go without being spotted. When she can afford to splurge she orders in and plates the meal herself, saving half for the next day, and puts on one of those ambient cafe noise streams so that she can pretend she's out.

Hiyoko PRO has paid the restaurant to allow a morning shoot behind locked doors, during what should have been the cooks' prep hours. They'll wrap well before the lunch rush hits. It's just Rei, Kosaka, two camera operators, and three chefs behind the counter, but she can feel the pressure of the thousands of views the video will garner. They might as well be here with her. She pretends

she can down huge portions despite her frame. The
internet likes to see her eat rich things, sweet things, heavy
things, even though they could get all those treats for
themselves anytime. So she orders tonkotsu ramen with
corn and butter, even though she would have preferred
shōyu, and smiles for the camera. The owner of the shop
leans over the counter and they chat like old friends. He
pulls pints of nama beer for all of them, even the women
behind the camera. Rei hopes that the sound of the
camerawomen laughing won't get edited out later. It's the
realest thing here.

The whole room goes quiet when a chef plunks the
steaming bowl, bigger than her head, down in front of her.
Rei adds a dash of ra-yu and a few spoonfuls of roasted
garlic chips from the little glass jar on the counter. Then
she claps her hands in front of her like a good girl and digs
in with chopsticks and spoon. Her calorie meter pings an
alarm as soon as she takes her first bite, reacting to the
creamy slide of fat over her tongue. She tries to ignore
it—closes her eyes, smiles as she chews—but faint panic
is rising in the back of her throat. It's the richest thing
she's had in weeks, far heavier than her 200-yen conbini
puddings. Her stomach roils and growls, and she doesn't
know whether it's a protest or an unruly plea for more.

As soon as the cameras stop Kosaka takes the bowl
away. He doesn't even finish her meal for her. He just
picks out the best bits of narutomaki and fatty char siu
pork and leaves the rest.

▶

SHE IS STILL fighting nausea when the car pulls up in
front of the KaruAni studio. The final segment they'll
film today will take her fans behind the scenes of *Entropy
Fighter Mizuki*. Of course Rei has met the producer, the
director, the sound director—but she's never talked to the

storyboarders or animators before.

She doesn't totally understand the premise, but she can't admit to it at this point; she's been smiling and nodding along for months now. Entropy Fighter Mizuki is supposedly a sci-fi magical girl powered by a perpetual motion machine, but that doesn't really tell Rei what the story is *about*: love or justice or betrayal or friendship.

Well, it's still a magical girl show, she reasons. It's probably about all of those things, and also extremely elaborate transformation sequences.

The senior key animator, Yonezu, meets them in the lobby. His hair and shirt are theatrically rumpled, and Rei wonders meanly how long it took him to set the wrinkles around his rolled cuffs to emphasize his forearms just so. He guides Rei and her staff through a warren of elevators and stairs and security doors. By the time they reach Studio B Rei is no longer sure what floor she's on.

She'd pictured rows of light tables and a library silence as the animators sketched. Instead, each of the desks jammed into neat, tight rows bears dual monitors. The animators raise their voices to be heard over the whirring and grinding of the computers' overworked fans. The air conditioner is doing its best, but the room is at least five degrees hotter than the hallway. A large screen on the wall displays a turnaround reference of Mizuki's model and color swatches for various lighting conditions.

"Right now our intermedia arts specialists are working on some upcoming fight sequences," Yonezu explains, looking at the camera instead of at Rei. "We're following these storyboards."

Rei gazes up at the huge sketches covering the walls. "Is it really okay for us to see these?"

"We posted them on socmed a few days ago, so it's nothing secret."

Driving hype, seeking validation: these are all things Rei understands. She nods sagely and tries to distract him before he figures out that she doesn't recognize any of these characters except Mizuki herself. "I've never been to an animation studio before. Can you explain what everyone's doing?"

When she cheats toward the camera she catches Kosaka signaling Yonezu. Kosaka has already picked out the animator he deems most photogenic and waves them over.

Rei leans over the animator's shoulder to watch him manipulating the models in a 3D engine, her curls swinging into his peripheral vision. He's deforming them, exaggerating the sizes of their fists and feet, squashing and stretching to create the illusion of perspective. Mizuki's hand grows, filling the screen, blotting out the model's face.

It takes Rei a moment to recenter herself. She has to remind herself that she is not Mizuki. It is not her body being manipulated in this funhouse mirror of unreality. She reaches inside to recover her perkiness and produces a credible smile, chirping, "Oh, I know what that is! I used to play around with Avidance in high school!"

"It's just called Avid now," the animator says. Rei pulls back to make room for him to scoot his chair out. He turns toward her to keep talking. "All the backgrounds are—"

"Wait." Kosaka steps in to correct the angle of the chair, making sure the animator's face is properly shown. Rei takes advantage of the pause to sneak a look at the employee ID hanging from his neck: Sai.

When the scene has been adjusted to Kosaka's satisfaction, he motions for them to carry on. Sai starts over. "All the backgrounds are hand-painted, but we use Avid for most of the character animations."

"That's so cool. I thought people only used Avid to make music videos with their avatars."

"Yeah, a lot of people do that. You've seen LYRICO's videos, right? This is the same software AventureP uses for those. And ZawaP uses this to make videos for Mizore. It's pretty much the standard."

"Mizore is a digital idol too, right? I think I've heard of her."

Sai narrows his eyes at her. "They're called Advanced Media Creation Girls."

"Since when?" Rei stifles an incredulous laugh, trying to project sincerity and interest. But she's been watching these videos for close to a decade, she's got three years of experience with older visions of Avidance, and she's never heard that term.

"Since they came out, but people keep calling them idols anyway." Sai's shrug rattles the enamel pins on his lanyard. "I guess I see the parallels. They're built the same way idols are, right? The producer chooses their look and their sound and makes them move."

Something in her flinches. She knows herself to be a built thing, but she has some input into her own construction. She didn't spring fully-formed from Kosaka's brain. Rei chooses another angle to parry from. "And why is it Advanced Media Creation *Girls*? People make music through other avatars too."

"You know why." A tall, tired woman rises from the desk behind Sai's to answer Rei. "Think how fast you can design an avatar, and then think about the turnover rate for female idols. People say 'girl' when they want a polite euphemism for 'disposable.'"

Kosaka will cut this bit out. He'd never post it. But Rei likes this woman with the immediacy of a splash of cold water to the face: her forthrightness and her rightness. Instead of playing to Sai and Yonezu, to Kosaka, to the cameras, she turns her attention to the woman.

"But digital idols last forever," she said. "They don't get old or injured or tired out. Some of them have stayed popular for decades." Of course, the longest-lived are fully digital, their voices built out of sound banks. Who knows where masks like LYRICO go, if the producer voicing them can't carry on?

"Some wines have a longer shelf life, but they only end two ways. They get drunk up or they turn into vinegar someday." The woman looks at Rei with a frank sympathy she's unused to.

"Rei," Kosaka says. "Mr. Sai was telling you about *Mizuki* before we were interrupted."

She tenses, but the woman tips her an abrupt nod and sits back down.

"So like I was saying, we use this for all the character animations," Sai begins. He's trying to find the rhythm of the conversation again. It's Rei's job here to help him, play to him so that he can show off his knowledge.

"It's so cool! Can you show me how to make her move?"

The world has been righted; she has put him in charge by appealing to his expertise. He demonstrates the controls, largely unchanged from Avidance, and Rei pretends smilingly not to know them.

She thinks she hears the tall woman laugh scornfully as she praises Sai. Kosaka will cut that out too.

▶

REI IS SO wrung-out that she falls asleep in the car on the way back to Hiyoko PRO. She wakes as Kosaka is parking in the underground garage, surprised and disoriented. She hasn't fallen asleep in front of him in months. At some point she stopped trusting him enough to allow herself that vulnerability.

They take the elevator up, Rei still blinking at the influx of light. Kosaka rests his hand on the small of her back, guiding her forward. She wishes he wouldn't.

"Since you had a nap," he says, "I bet you can do one more video today. Let's go up to the streaming studio and do a choreography tutorial. I can hold the camera. Go change and freshen up."

Rei can't quite squash the suspicion that this was his plan all along, and he just didn't bother to clue her in. She's used to having one more task tacked onto her list at the last minute; she's used to saying yes. When she returns to Kosaka's desk on the fourth floor, redone as if to restart the day, Aimi is there. Still wearing her school uniform, she sits curled into a corner of the couch, a textbook open in her lap and her lips moving as she drags a finger along the page.

"Hi," Rei chirps. "You came straight from school?"

Aimi nods. "I quit my club activities. Mr. Kosaka says I won't have time once I debut."

Their shared manager is nowhere to be seen, despite the open floor plan. "Where is Mr. Kosaka?" Rei asks, making sure to attach the honorific. She knows better than to speak of him the way she thinks of him.

"Upstairs. Someone pulled him into a meeting—I don't know who, but they looked like they were in a hurry."

Rei hesitates.

She could sit with Aimi, keep trying to build this strange and fragile rapport with the child, see if perhaps they might ally themselves to share the burdens Kosaka loads onto their frail shoulders.

Or she could grab the chair from the vacant desk next to Kosaka's and wheel it next to his seat just as she always does, reasserting her position: closest to him, his top priority.

Safely curled onto her throne, Rei straightens her back and asks Aimi, "Do you know when your debut will be?" Kosaka has abandoned a cup of coffee on his desk; she picks it up just to give her hands something to do and sips at it. It's miserable stuff, old and stale and bitter, and her tinted lip balm leaves a berry-pink print on the rim like she's tagging her turf.

Aimi scrunches up her face. "Not exactly. But soon, I think? Mr. Kosaka gave me the demo for my first single today, but he says we'll release it for limited streaming play and radio before it actually goes on sale."

"That's normal," Rei says. "I was promoting my first single on webcasts and TV for a whole month before it even came out. Hey, I'd like to hear the demo, if that's okay?"

Aimi darts to her side, smart in hand. "I was hoping you'd ask!" She beams at Rei. "It's really nice of you to take so much interest in me, even though I'm just a newbie. Or is it because I'm competition?"

The words echo hollow in Rei's middle ear as she realizes that Aimi is much sharper than she'd thought. She can feel her eardrums quivering.

"I don't want us to compete," she says carefully. "After all, we have the same manager. It's better business for me to promote you. If we're both popular, it's good for the agency as a whole."

"I know that. But I wasn't sure you knew it, from how you looked at me." Aimi shrugs a little and starts the track queued up on her smart's music app.

As bright, sparkling synths blare from the device, Rei says, "I was surprised. I'm sorry if you thought I was unfriendly, or—"

"I didn't think you were unfriendly. I thought you were scared of me."

The sound of singing saves Rei from having to reply. She knows this voice. The memory is faraway but she is certain.

"This is Yukarin," she says.

Aimi nods. "She didn't ever release it, because... you know. Kosaka said I could have it. What do you think?"

What Rei thinks is, why has Kosaka been sitting on this for four years? Why didn't he give this song to me?

She knows she's being unfair. Her brand image is totally different from Yukarin's. Yukarin debuted at fifteen and was kept an eternal Cinderella, half her songs a bright-eyed bubblegum technopop celebration of how happy she was just to be onstage. She lived inside the faux surprise of a pageant queen. Rei knows a lot of her own songs are pedestrian, but at least she's got more range and substance than that.

She is jealous anyway. Secrets, she's beginning to
think, are a one-way street in this relationship. Kosaka's
squashed the secrets out of her, but he holds his close.

Aimi is still waiting for her answer and looking at her.
A pang of déjà vu shoots through Rei.

"It's good," she says, "and I think it's just right for you.
What's it called?"

"'Cendrillon Dreaming.'"

It's a Yukarin song right to the title. Rei wrinkles her
nose despite herself.

"I want to change it," Aimi says a little sheepishly. "But..."
"But?"

"I don't think I can ask Mr. Kosaka for that. Not yet,
anyway."

"I don't think I could either," Rei admits. Remembering
that they're in public, she adds, "And besides, I wouldn't. He
knows best." The closest manager is at a desk three meters
away, talking on the phone, but she won't take the risk. Still,
the lie leaves a sour taste in her mouth. The least she could
do is try to warn Aimi, but would she even be believed?

Somehow Rei doubts it.

"Of course he does. And I fit the Cinderella image for
now anyway. Normal schoolgirl becomes a star." Aimi
shrugs diffidently. "That's premature of me, but."

The only right answer is to reassure her, and Rei tries.
"Well, of course you'll be a star."

"People will like me just for being young, but it'll be a
problem later. It's going to be hard to change my image
once I'm established. We'll play off each other well,
though. You have kind of a diva image, but being around
me makes you look like a sexy big sister type and then I'm
even more cute and innocent in comparison."

Oh, she is clever. Against all her better judgment Rei
smiles like she hasn't in a long time: not calculated to
dazzle or to entice, not to elicit a reaction, but just to
communicate her own delight.

Aimi smiles back. Rei had forgotten the fizz and spark of being in cahoots, the way conspiracy gets all the way up into her sinuses like ramune chugged on a sunny day.

"I'd like us to be friends," Aimi said. "It's strange and hard trying to trick the whole world into loving you. And none of my school friends will ever really understand that, and I probably won't get to spend very much time with other idols here for a while, so I think we should at least try to like each other."

Later, Rei will understand that this is courage. Right now it is only bewildering. She doesn't know anything about this kind of earnest courage. Her own is the sort that clenches its teeth and death-marches endlessly forward in pursuit of goals she's long since stopped wanting, just because she's committed herself to the cause.

Despite that, she says, "I don't think I'll need to try very hard."

This is all she has time to say before Kosaka returns to drag her upstairs to film, but Aimi's smile sticks in her head the rest of the day.

"HOLD STILL," REI whispered. Ririko closed her eyes, smiling when Rei flicked the brush over her eyelids, leaving bronze glitter in its wake. Rei pretended not to notice the cameras and chose another brush. Ririko laughed at the ticklish touch of eyeliner. When she shook Rei's hand jumped, the dark line of gel smearing into the creases at the outer corner of Ririko's eyes.

"Ah! Sorry."

"Cut!" the director shouted.

"Sorry, it was my fault for laughing," Ririko said. "I ruined the take."

"I feel a little silly," Rei admitted as she turned towards the vanity table to check her own face in the mirror.

The set was styled to look like a dressing room, with the premise of the commercial being that Venus Versus was getting ready to go onstage. Every surface gleamed sterile white as the black swarms of cameras orbited the girls. "Every time I put makeup on you I'm covering up an actual professional's work."

Kosaka joined them, tucking his smart back into his pocket and scrubbing a hand through his hair. "Doing okay, girls? The director says once we get this shot we're done."

"Can you ask them to turn the air conditioning off?" Rei asked. "It's really cold here." Their costumes did nothing to shield them from the blasts of cold air: fluffy white chiffon blouses cut off the shoulder, anchored by short voluminous skirts in signature Sunny Labo yellow.

Kosaka frowned down at her. Abruptly he shed his blazer and draped it over her narrow shoulders, and strode away to speak with the director. The silk lining still held the heat of his body, and Rei tugged it more tightly around herself.

"Okay," Ririko said, clearly steeling herself. "I promise not to ruin this one. But it really does tickle."

"Too bad we can't go back to Avidance," Rei joked. "I could just download the pattern and then choose your color on the slider."

"Would the dance scenes have been easier in Avidance too?" Ririko teased. They'd spent the whole morning filming the dance shots. The director had wanted to get those out of the way while the girls were still fresh.

"Probably!" Rei stretched out her right leg and wiggled her ankle. The joint popped loudly. She'd stumbled on it earlier, but at least it didn't look swollen. "Nothing a hot bath tonight won't fix, though."

Kosaka returned to them, whisking his jacket off Rei's shoulders. Her arms, exposed, prickled with goosebumps. "They'll turn off the air conditioning," he reported. "And we're changing up the shot. Since Ririko can't hold still while you do her eyes, Rei, we won't bother. We'll use the footage of her doing your eyes, and you can just paint Ririko's cheeks and lips."

He signaled for Sunny Labo's makeup artist to intervene. Rei watched Ririko's small, pearly teeth digging into her bottom lip but, to her credit, she held perfectly still as they applied her eyeshadow and liner.

"Places!" the director shouted. Rei picked up the limited edition summer makeup palette and selected a fluffy brush from the tray on the table. She faced Ririko, smiling, as "OVER HORIZON" blared through the set. The song would actually be added in post-production, but the director had insisted on playing it to capture the mood.

"You know," Ririko said, "out of all our songs so far, this one is my favorite."

Rei leaned closer, drawn in by the gravitational force of Ririko's smile, the warmth rising off her skin, her faint perfume of peonies and honey.

"Mine too," she said.

伍

"**O**NTO THE SCALE, please."

Rei bites back her sigh, producing a credible imitation of an obliging smile. The exam room is always too cold. She shivers in the t-shirt and thin sweatpants she always wears for checkups.

Office staff, Rei has heard, are only subjected to this indignity once a year. As a Hiyoko PRO idol, she has to undergo an occupational health examination and stress check every month; it's right there in her contract. It's only been three weeks since she was last here. Rei suspects that Kosaka has moved it up to punish her for missing her salon appointment.

Kosaka is standing on the other side of the polyplastic curtain, and Dr. Makino raises her voice for his benefit. "43.72 kilos."

"Rei," he says, and she doesn't need to hear any more to parse the reprimand in his voice.

She'd like to tell him to shut up. She absolutely won't, of course. Rei is lucky that his interest in her body is purely clinical, analytical, like the owner of a prize thoroughbred determined to see the beast keep winning. She's overheard other idols whisper backstage about managers whose interest is more personal. For all Kosaka's tantrums and moods, at least he has never demanded that kind of quid pro quo. It could be so much worse.

She asked herself once what she would do if ever his interest was less than professional. She still doesn't have an answer, but she has her career to think of. She can't risk being labeled difficult to work with.

Then again, everyone remembers how Yasumoto Reina's producer forced her to quit her unit after she married him.

She curls her hand into a fist until her nails bite into her palm and steps down to let the doctor check her three sizes. There's supposedly some kind of medical reason her hip-to-waist ratio matters, but Rei suspects the main reason the company cares about it is for costume fittings.

And, of course, her three sizes are posted online on her agency profile. This is ostensibly to make it easier for casting agents to scout her. She's gotten a couple bit parts and guest spots in Monday-night dramas before. Career utility notwithstanding, she's burdened with the unfortunate awareness that some of her fans are interested in that information for more prurient reasons. Either way, making her numbers public obligates her to maintain them. Her fans might feel misled if any discrepancy ever became public knowledge.

She hates that they have the power to make her police herself like this—that they can make her hate herself. But maybe she's only shifting the blame. Maybe she'd still be this strict and unforgiving with herself left to her own devices.

The doctor draws two vials of blood, leaving Rei's head spinning when she tries to stand. She drops back onto the padded examination bench.

"Sorry, sorry," Rei says. "I know it's an inconvenience, but can I have a minute?"

The doctor sighs and fetches out a single biscuit, wrapped in clear bioplastic, from a tin on her desk. "Here.

You'll feel better if you eat something."

Hypocrite, Rei doesn't say. Dr. Makino is so careful to give herself plausible deniability. She will hand Rei a 47-kcal cookie when she's woozy, but she's never once asked Rei when her last period was. She installed all the bioapps that track Rei's nutritional intake, but she doesn't double-check the alarm thresholds that Kosaka set. She writes Rei prescriptions for water pills and herbal laxatives. She's really only here so that Hiyoko PRO can pretend they're doing their due diligence. Rei doesn't know what the doctor would even do if something was found to be wrong with her. Would Kosaka—or the people who pay him—really allow her to pause her activities to recover?

Looking at the doctor, Rei realizes it's probably not even fair to call Dr. Makino a hypocrite. She's nearly as slim as Rei, though the white coat hides that fact at a glance. What strictures does the doctor subject herself to? Is her regimen as harsh as Rei's, all those hours of cardio broken up by doses of nutrient jelly in lieu of meals?

You chose it, Rei reminds herself. You chose it, so deal with it. You chose it, so you don't get to complain. You said you'd do anything to be an idol, to be loved—now prove it.

So she stands up and lets Dr. Makino swab cold gel onto her and affix the electrodes for her electrocardiogram, trying not to tremble all the while. The weight of the wires trailing off her chest and wrists and ankles and the sense of confinement make her want to retch. But Rei has always struggled to throw up, even when she's trying to, so keeping the bile down isn't hard.

Dr. Makino's hands are so gentle. Rei lets her detach the electrodes and wipe the gel away, and doesn't even wriggle. Hours of costume fittings have accustomed her to strange and unwanted hands. The doctor guides her to the tiny X-ray booth in the corner. She talks Rei through her breathing as the machine clicks away.

When they are done Rei pulls her arms in like a turtle and wiggles her bra back on under her t-shirt. "All clear?" she asks, eager to be done with it.

"How are you feeling today?" Dr. Makino asks. She opens the curtain and returns to her desk, nodding to Kosaka, who leans waiting by the door.

"Fine," Rei lies.

"No headaches? Trouble sleeping?" She's looking at her computer, not at Rei.

"No," she lies.

"Good." And the doctor turns to Kosaka. "Well, I'm counting on you to take care of her."

REI IS RUTHLESS in the practice rooms, but no one is supposed to know that except Kosaka and the string of choreographers and trainers he hires. Yet Aimi is here now; Aimi is watching Rei lean against the wall, breathing hard as she pins a sweaty curl back up.

Aimi has a little tact about it; she faces the big mirror that takes up the far wall of the room and watches Rei's pained reflection instead of the real thing. This is not a comfort for Rei, whose stomach gurgles. She always waits to eat until after dance lessons. Better the dizziness of working herself on an empty stomach than the sight of her bloated belly in the mirror.

Ms. Kaida, today's choreographer, doesn't take it any easier on Aimi than she does Rei. Aimi only has one song so far, but that's even more reason why her performance has to be perfect. Rei stretches, rubs her sore shoulder, and watches Aimi's slender arms arc through the air.

When the song ends, Aimi doubles over, hands on her knees. It's not a technically strenuous routine but she's done it three times in less than fifteen minutes now. Rei grabs a bottle of Pocari Sweat and holds it out to Aimi.

"You'll build up stamina pretty soon," she says. "Don't worry."

Aimi laughs as though she's embarrassed. "I feel a little sick." She accepts the bottle and presses it to her sweaty forehead to cool herself down.

"Did you eat lunch?"

"Yeah."

"I made that mistake too at first," Rei says. "Wait until after practice next time."

"Don't you get hungry?" Aimi asks.

Rei shrugs. "I'm used to it."

"Enough slacking," Ms. Kaida calls out. "Rei, let me see 'Miracle♡Heartscape.' That's on your set list for your next live, isn't it?"

"Yes ma'am!" Rei gives Aimi a little push towards the yoga mats stacked at the back of the room. "Go catch your breath."

Ms. Kaida drills her on the refrain without music, counting off the beats, until Rei loses track of how many times she's done it. Her arm motions are large, simple, and repetitive, so that the audience can join in with penlights and cyalumes. "Exaggerate it more," Ms. Kaida instructs. "The audience needs to understand exactly where you'll move next or else they can't keep up."

Rei catches sight of Aimi in the mirror, her hands up, following along with a smile on her face. Rei can't help grinning back.

"Yes! That's it," Ms. Kaida says, and makes her run through the song in its entirety twice before she lets the girls trade off again.

Rei watches the frustration build on Aimi's face as Ms. Kaida restarts "Cendrillon Dreaming" over and over, finally dispensing with the music entirely to chant the eight-count herself, clapping on the beat. She could tell Aimi it gets easier, but that would be a lie. The better Rei gets, the less she satisfies anyone, herself included. There is always a

more challenging song looming on the horizon. All success
does is raise the bar higher.

But if Aimi is anything like Rei she will feed off this.
She will live for it. Rei suspects that people who know how
to be satisfied with themselves don't become idols.

There is no clock in the dance studio. Ms. Kaida
will let them go when their time is up, and if she doesn't
Kosaka will come collect them. Rei doesn't even try to
peek at Ms. Kaida's wristwatch anymore.

She dances through "Mirror Fracture" twice before
Aimi is put to her trial again. This time it's Rei's turn to
follow along from the back of the room, if only to vent her
nervous energy. Her eyes meet Aimi's in the mirror and she
smiles to encourage the girl. She hopes Aimi isn't as sick of
"Cendrillon Dreaming" as she is. Rei is sure she's watched it
enough that she could perform the whole thing herself now.

"Rei, your turn," Ms. Kaida calls. The opening notes of
"Hybrid Heart" set all of Rei's sixty trillion cells on fire, and
she darts to the center of the practice floor as Aimi falls back.

The recording is the one Kosaka deemed acceptable,
but Rei's own lyrics are playing in her head. She's sung
them to herself in the shower, hummed them as she puts
on her makeup. She plays back the voice memo in her
headphones when she takes the train to the office. The
words are a part of her DNA now. She's even thought
about booting up her old copy of Avidance to make her
doll dance to it.

But wouldn't doing it for real be a million times better
than just running through it virtually?

Rei follows Ms. Kaida's moves, but her mind is racing
into the future. If she did it live, made the song her own
in front of her fans, Kosaka couldn't stop her. He would
never risk ruining the show. And if they loved it—*when*
they loved it, because she'd be offering them the taste of
real vulnerability they all craved—he'd have to admit
she'd been right. Rei can show him that she understands

what people want from her, and how to make them believe they're getting it. She needs to convince Kosaka that what he needs is a *partner*, not a prisoner. She has to rise to his level.

She could do it. She could show him that she could be a partner to him instead of just a doll. And if he accepted her as his equal she could stay at Hiyoko PRO with him, resent him less, keep being an idol, keep being Aimi's senior. Maybe she could even help Aimi, protect her from the worst of Kosaka's moods.

Rei had never understood that Ririko needed to be protected until it was already too late. She won't let herself make that mistake with Aimi.

WHEN REI DREAMS now, it's of LYRICO in her white dress, singing alone in the black void of an unrendered environment. She has watched the video so often that she knows every coquettish tilt of LYRICO's chin by heart. AventureP was responding to her with that post, she's sure of it. To write it off as pareidolia would just be lying to herself.

It's not some failure of pattern recognition. She's not just manufacturing meaning in her coincidences. There is a message here, if only she can decipher it.

She wakes in the night to find herself half mumbling the lyrics to "OVER HORIZON." She still knows it by heart. Rei doesn't forget lyrics.

She could send a message back. That's the whole point of the internet, right? All that data is just communication.

A couple hundred people have responded to her post: fans sharing what their own favorite V^2 song was, or reminiscing about past concerts, or telling her how much stronger a singer she's become since going solo. They want her to acknowledge them, clamoring for her attention, even if it's just a single tap on the "like" button.

But AventureP went further than that. AventureP reached out and offered up their voice.

And, a little voice inside her whispers, the only person who would ever have any reason to do that would be Ririko.

Well, that's not true. AventureP could be some obsessive superfan, a front-row manager crowding people back, the kind of fan who's going to use the tiny reflections in Rei's pupils to track her location when she posts selfies. Maybe AventureP is just waiting for their chance to break into Rei's mailbox and steal her pension slips or her gas bill.

But couldn't it be Ririko?

She wants so badly for it to be Ririko.

She feels blindly for her smart on the nightstand. The darkness dissipates abruptly as the device comes to life in a blue-white glow, so sharp that it sets her vision sparking and fuzzing.

She goes to AventureP's NeuroDouga profile; she's been there so often that she only needs to put in three letters before it autocompletes.

This user has disabled direct messages.

Undaunted, Rei moves on to her various social scrolls, but every service turns up the same result: this user has disabled direct messages. AventureP is a walled city with no way for Rei to slip in, no way to to slide a message past the guards. The best she could do would be tagging AventureP in a post of her own, like pinning her letter to a door.

She returns to NeuroDouga, considering: "Alice Underground" is the most famous of LYRICO's songs at over 13 million views, but Rei's real favorite is "Let's Meet at the Station Gate." There's something about its driving bassline that makes her put it on repeat for hours at a time, as AventureP's voice pleads from under LYRICO's mask, asking her lover to wake from their frozen dreams and rejoin the real world.

Her old headset is still crammed in a desk drawer. She hauls it out and hooks it up to her laptop. She barely uses her computer anymore; she does all her social media on her phone, and her career doesn't leave much time for hobbies like gaming or making videos. But it's the same laptop she's had since she was a student, and it still has audio editing software on it.

She knows "Let's Meet at the Station Gate" front and back, as well as she knows any of her own songs. She doesn't need to look up the lyrics to sing the A-melo and the hook as sweetly and feelingly as she can. She's building a world with her voice, one that has just enough room for Ririko and herself, AventureP and herself, to hold this song shimmering between them.

It's only when she's listening to the playback that she realizes she can't possibly post this to her own account. Kosaka has shut down that avenue entirely. If he saw something like this pass through his review queue he'd never let her out of his sight again. She shouldn't even have used her smart to look at AventureP's profiles. What will she say if Kosaka asks about it?

He knows every calorie that passes her lips, every video that hits her eyes. He might not know what she dreams of, but he certainly knows how often she dreams: one of her bioapps breaks down exactly how long she spends in every stage of sleep. The only real privacy she has is in her thoughts, and sometimes she's not sure of even that.

She drums her fingers against the shell of the laptop, blue nitrogels thudding a dull rhythm. Its fan whirs quietly, just audible over her air conditioner. It isn't loud enough to be alarming yet; she could open another program without overtaxing the RAM.

She opens the browser and begins scanning her bookmarks, frowning over websites she hasn't logged into for years. Surely there's something she could recycle.

After a moment she turns up an abandoned social

scroll, one she'd used back in high school. User 0karastart is as close as she can get to an anonymous account; she never posted a selfy or #今日のコーデ without first blotting out her face with a sticker or an emoji, she never used her real name, and she stopped posting to it a month before she even moved to Tokyo so that she could truthfully say she wasn't on socmed. She had topped out at a whopping twenty-one followers, mostly classmates she was on friendly terms with and a couple of bots. Now she has eight, all of them apparently inactive.

One of them, she realizes as she scans the list, is Ririko's abandoned account. The last login was over four years ago. The profile picture isn't even of Ririko herself. It's a cropped bit of a panel from Hyperdimensional Ark Northern Blue, an insufferably convoluted sci-fi manga.

All the same, Rei's heart twists. She misses seeing that ridiculous picture pop up every time Ririko messaged her. She misses staying up way too late to chat, even though they'll see each other at school tomorrow, because there are some conversations that can only happen at 26:00 on the other side of a screen, in that liminal space where the calendar day and the lived day fork away from each other into a technical Wednesday and a long, long Tuesday.

There is something between a sob and a sigh caught in the hollow under her ribcage. She does not let it out.

She turns her mind from Ririko and clicks the icon for "new post." She uploads her file, writes a message, deletes it.

She taps in another message and deletes that too.

Finally she types out her favorite line from "Let's Meet at the Station Gate": "We're nothing but wounds all over, but we can start from here." She tags AventureP and hits "post" before she can talk herself out of it. Every one of her vertebrae loosens in the sudden flood of relief. Her jaw clicks as it relaxes.

Muscle memory compelling her, she tabs back over

to her direct messages and stares at Ririko's account at the top of the list. The preview shows Ririko's last reply before they'd continued the conversation on some different platform: But wouldn't you rather be a witch than a princess? Witches can transform things, after all.

She opens the conversation, wondering what she had said to provoke a response like that.

I don't care if they laugh at us for being dolls. Being an idol is half a game of dress-up anyway. They'll treat us like we're princesses, and if they do it long enough it's as good as true.

Rei marvels at how she could have been so sharp and yet so profoundly foolish at seventeen. Yes, she is treated like a princess now: surveilled, controlled, muzzled, every move calculated in advance. She'd thought back then that she'd be in on the joke, pulling the proverbial strings. But in the end, she is no better than Yukarin. She thinks fleetingly of Aimi planning how to manage her image, as if Kosaka will let her.

She hovers over the empty reply field, chewing her lower lip.

I finally realized you were right, she types. It would have been better to be a witch. I'm sorry. I wish I could see you again.

She hits sends, a pained howl into the abyss, and waits. Eventually she falls asleep in front of the screen, still waiting for the message to mark itself read.

Ririko's reply never comes. But when she wakes up in the morning, stiff-necked, head throbbing, AventureP has liked her post.

▶

Days in television don't start as early as most people expect, at least not for an idol. Rei doesn't have to be at the TV station until 13:00, an hour before filming starts. She has time to make up some of last night's missed sleep before she meets Kosaka and Aimi at the office.

Aimi's chatter keeps Rei so entertained in the car
that she doesn't notice Kosaka's silence at first. When
at last she picks up on it, she watches first his profile
as he worries at his lower lip with his teeth, then as his
forehead creases in the rearview mirror. He looks tired.
He's only ten years older than Rei—she'd thought he was
so young and handsome when they first met, and basked
in his praise—but he holds himself as though he has four
decades and a hip replacement on her.

She knows better than to feel sorry for him. She tries so
hard to practice not feeling sorry for him, but—

Is she why he looks so tired? When did those shadows
settle in under his eyes? Are those her fault too, or are
these the artifacts of Yukarin?

He catches her eye when he checks the mirror to merge
left and Rei startles at the sweetness of the smile he gives
her. He is still handsome, even though she knows now how
ugly his moods can turn. She forces an answering smile.

He doesn't need to say "good girl" anymore when
she smiles for him. He used to, when she'd just started
her solo career, and she'd understood the implicit
comparison to Ririko in his praise. But she is trained
now. Keeping the praise intermittent makes her try
harder to earn it. She understands his tactics perfectly
but the knowledge does nothing to immunize her awful,
craving brain.

Aimi is enchanted by the TV station's bustle and
clamor, the jungles of wires, the more famous celebrities
hurrying past them in the halls with heels clicking.
She seizes Rei's arm and keeps up a frantic running
commentary in her ear: "Oh! It's one of the guys from
HIGH BEAT! And look, over there, isn't that Nitta
Mitsuko? Incredible!"

Rei stifles a laugh into her hand. "Don't look right at
them! It's rude. And they'll all know you're new."

"I am new. Why do I have to pretend I'm not?"

"If we're unprofessional it'll make Mr. Kosaka look bad for not training us properly."

Aimi giggles. "Okay, okay! I won't look, But we just passed another of those boys from HIGH BEAT and he looked right at you. Do you think they're cute?"

"I haven't really paid any attention to them." Rei shrugs. A boy band isn't direct competition, and therefore beneath her notice. "Are their songs good?"

"Who cares? They don't need to be good, with faces like that."

The words sting, even when aimed at someone else. Rei's been on the sharp end of them too many times to hear them neutrally.

"That's what people say about us, too," she says, careful to keep her voice low. Kosaka is only two steps in front of them.

"So? They're not wrong," Aimi says. "We're so pretty that we don't need to be good. But we are anyway, and that's what makes us special."

Rei doesn't know how to disagree. She wants to think that her skill matters. Sure, she can have fans solely on the strength of her face, but doesn't she have more because of how well she sings and dances? A talentless hack screeching into the mic wouldn't sell as many downloads.

She wonders whether AventureP ever worries about LYRICO this way. Does the beauty of their digital face matter? Can AventureP say with confidence that their songs are what the fans value?

"Will you help me with my hair?" Aimi asks as they head for the dressing room.

"Help you do what? It's already perfect." Kosaka would be furious if Rei tried to curl Aimi's hair. It'd ruin the contrast between them.

"My makeup, then!"

Rei has seen Aimi put makeup on. She does a perfectly good job on her own. She doesn't need the help.

She just wants to be cared for.

So Rei puts on her own makeup first and coils her hair into a clip to put a little more bounce into her curls, and turns her hands to Aimi. Aimi will not voice her anxiety but the way she arches into Rei's touch says it all. Rei brushes out Aimi's long, silky black hair and dabs blush and lip gloss onto her fine-featured face. When Aimi joins in, matching her note for note, Rei realizes that she's been humming "OVER HORIZON."

Rei cuts herself off and asks, "Ready?"

"I am now," Aimi says.

Kosaka has waited for them outside the dressing room, and escorts them to the soundstage: a cozy talk show setup with overstuffed couches and an array of wall-mounted screens behind them. The studio audience breaks into a chorus of astonished "eeeeeeeehh's" when they enter.

They're overselling it, Rei thinks. Studio audience members are paid, but not that well. Why put in so much effort before the cameras even start rolling? Still, she tosses them a smile and a little wave, curling her fingers. Aimi is quick to imitate her, setting off a round of excited whispers. Who is this pretty mystery girl?

"Doing okay, Aimi?" Kosaka mutters, repositioning himself to shield her from the audience's prying eyes. "Remember, just like we rehearsed. Don't jump in too fast to answer their questions. Stay cheerful no matter what they ask. Don't stop smiling for them."

"I will," Aimi promises.

"Good girl." He pats her head briefly. Rei averts her eyes, regretting all over again any thought she'd ever had of leaving. Who would look after Aimi? Kosaka will not be this kind to her forever. *Good* is a placeholder word he uses because *obedient* has too many syllables, and he doesn't register any difference in definition.

Finally the set is shouted to silence, the cameras go live, and they are called to the stage. The glare of the lights wipes out all but the first two rows of the audience. When

Rei squeeze's Aimi's hand, whispers to her that there's
nothing to worry about, she's talking to her past self as
much as Aimi, as though her voice could reach through
time to soothe the Rei of V², eighteen and trembling.

TRIUMPH SANG THROUGH Rei's veins and she would have
held onto that exhilaration forever if only she could.
In this mood she could have kept going for hours. She
wanted to sing more, dance more, but she knew the rules.
She and Ririko, still under twenty, would be driven home
by Kosaka, forced to skip their own afterparty so that
the staff could drink freely without fear of causing them a
scandal.

But first: the debriefing.

"We did well tonight, didn't we?" she hissed to Ririko
as they sat down, tulle petticoats crunching. Some tech
had thoughtfully arranged a circle of folding chairs.

Ririko sucked her lower lip between her teeth and
scraped her lip gloss. "Well, Mr. Kosaka will tell us."

Kosaka, clipboard tucked under his arm, joined
them. He handed each girl a Pocari Sweat. "Good job
out there," he said. The formulaic phrase did nothing to
reassure Rei.

The band and key crew trickled in, congratulating each
other on a job well done. They took their places in the
circle as the junior staff bustled around them: winding up
cords, collecting trash. A tech approached Rei and Ririko
to extract their microphones, untangling the headsets
from their sweaty hair and unclipping their transmitters
and battery packs.

"Thank you for all your hard work tonight, everyone!"
Kosaka clapped his hands to silence the room. Rei wondered
if they'd ever respect her and Ririko that way, falling
silent when they spoke. Everyone had been nice, but their

comparative inexperience—their first really big live, their
first time at this venue—made them the babies of the bunch
by far. She'd felt underfoot and in the way every time she'd
tried to ask questions, even with her own backing band.

"Congratulations on making it through in one piece.
Let's do this quickly so we can get the girls home. Rei, you
first. How do you think it went?"

"I was really nervous, but I was able to do my best
because everyone was here with me! And Ririko sang
really well, of course." She lowered her gaze. "I'm sorry
I came in too early for the C-melo on 'Starlit Nexus.' I'll
practice more and do better next time!" She bowed in the
direction of the band members, cheeks burning. They'd
caught her mistake and covered for her, but she was sure
the audience had seen her flinch.

"You did well during the songs, but you seemed a little
hesitant during the MC. Ririko did most of the talking."
Kosaka wasn't even looking at her, his eyes on his
clipboard. "You'll have to step up more next time."

"I will!"

"Ririko?"

She was silent for a long moment. Rei watched the
stillness of her profile, a little awed by that dignity.

"I think we did really well for our biggest live so far,"
Ririko said. "The audience seemed to really enjoy it,
and I had fun too. Next time I want to tighten up my
choreography. I know I was a little slow in some places."

"You look at your own hands too much when you dance,"
Kosaka said. "And you need to aim more of your eye
contact at the cameras and the audience, and less at Rei."

"Speaking of eye contact," Rei interrupted. She turned
to the bandmaster/keyboardist, Kitagawa, sitting on her
left. "Thank you for cueing me in for 'Fantasy Disco.' I
wasn't sure when I should come in."

"I could tell. You covered well, though." Kitagawa
looked to Kosaka as he went on, assuming permission

to talk. "Our rhythm was off on 'Blooming Star,' and it made it hard for the girls to keep up. We need to spend more time practicing that one."

"Noted," Kosaka said. But he wasn't done with Venus Versus, and refocused on them. "Ririko, you let your smile drop when you're not facing the audience. Don't forget that there are cameras behind you. As long as you're standing on that stage, you should be smiling."

Ririko acknowledged him with a quick nod. "Yes, of course. I'm sorry," she said. "I'll work harder next time."

"Try to connect with the audience more, like Rei does."

Rei's costume was glued to her skin with her own sweat, and she shifted in her seat, itchy. "The audience loves Ririko," she said, determined to show that Kosaka couldn't play them off each other. "They cheered so much louder for her solo than mine! I need to work harder." She flicked her eyes around the circle of chairs in time to catch the bassist wincing.

"Yours was amazing," Ririko cut in. She reached over to squeeze Rei's arm. "You were...the most *you* I've ever seen you somehow, dancing alone under that spotlight."

Rei flushed, soaking up the praise gladly. She'd been so nervous that she'd cried in the wings just before she ran on. The only thing that had given her enough courage to go out alone was the quick, fierce hug Ririko had closed around her when they crossed paths in the dark. "I—I just want to give the audience my best self."

"Good girl," Kosaka said, and patted her head.

Ririko's smile had gone tight again. "Just make sure you keep something back for yourself," she muttered.

The only version of herself that Rei has ever wanted to keep was the one reflected in Ririko's eyes. That Rei was so much bigger and nobler than the real thing. And yet it was a version of herself that she wanted to live up to, a Rei better worth being than Kosaka's obedient pet. There was no sensible way to say any of that and certainly no cool or cute one.

The moment passed. Kosaka had turned his attention to one of the lighting techs, whose follow spot hadn't kept pace with Rei as she ran onto a wing of the stage to get closer to the audience. Rei pulled at the hem of her costume again, trying vainly to make the scant silver skirt cover even a millimeter more of her exposed thighs. Ririko caught her hand again.

"Don't. It looks good," she murmured.

"Really? You like it?"

Rei had asked the wrong question again, with unerring precision. She knew it from Ririko's fractional pause.

"No," Ririko finally said, too proud to lie. "It suits you perfectly. It's stunning. But I don't like it."

Rei nodded as if she understood, unwilling to admit confusion. "Maybe Mr. Kosaka will let us have more input on the costumes next time. Well, at least we got to sing! He could give us maid costumes with cat ears, and I'd wear it, as long as we got to sing."

"Shhh. He'll hear you. Don't give him ideas." And the face that Ririko made, amused and horrified, wiped any spot of unease from Rei's mind.

陸

REI KNOWS THAT she should like cycloramas, or at least be neutral towards them. That curve of backdrop is full of possibility, after all: a thousand poses and expressions freed from the burden of context. But maybe she's just not imaginative enough to use the cyclorama properly, because she'd take the themed sets upstairs over it any day. Give her architecture and props to interact with and Rei can produce any number of charming scenes. In the blankness of the cyclorama she is dependent on the photographer calling for her to move and shift as they tweak the shutter and aperture and zoom levels.

"It's fun just watching you!" Aimi chirps, darting onto the set as the photographer pauses to adjust the camera again. "Rei, teach me to pose like you do. You have so much more experience, after all."

"I just do what the photographer tells me to," Rei says, flushing. A burst of clicks echoes through the studio, startling her.

"Nice!" the photographer calls out. "You two looked good together, just then."

"Oh, show me!" Aimi bounces away from Rei, her shoe leaving a small black scuff on the white floor. "Please, Mr. Hayasaka?"

He laughs indulgently and turns the camera to show her the preview window. Rei joins them, craning to peer over Aimi's shoulder.

The tiny Rei in the photo is cheated slightly towards the camera as if her body is trained to seek her best angles instinctively. She's blushing, lips slightly parted and her head dipped just enough to emphasize the delicate point of her chin. Aimi's face is tilted up towards her, innocent and adoring and just a little bit playful, her expression about to bloom into a laugh.

Anxiety lances through Rei, fierce enough to make her bite her lip. Is she going to be the serious, intense one now? It was always Ririko's job to temper Rei's cheekiness and energy with thoughtful pauses and to turn pink when Rei teased her.

As a solo idol she has to be everything in turns: spunky, playful, serious, sexy. That will be Aimi's job too, but Rei knows what a heavy load it is to carry. If she can lighten it when they are together by slotting herself into the "right" role, she can't justify refusing to show that kindness.

She meets Aimi's eyes, trying to call back the magic she shared with Ririko, that carbonated sensation of being in on a joke together. "Come pose with me. We're a team now, after all."

Kosaka, tucked into a corner of the room with the girls' purses piled next to him, looks up from his smart. "Don't forget that the point of this is to get shots we can sell. That means solos."

"Oh, can't we have a few together?" Rei pleads. "Maybe people who buy my bromides will want them just to have a complete set. And if I was in some of Aimi's pictures, maybe my fans would buy her photos too."

"Fine. No more than three of the final shots, though, so don't waste too much of Mr. Hayasaka's time on it. We need to move on to the sets for the photobook shots." Kosaka returns to his smart. She is dismissed.

"Yay!" Aimi skips towards the cyclorama, beaming. "Come on, Rei!"

Rei shoves away all her longing for Ririko and follows, pasting her smile back on. It's only going to be the whole rest of her day. She can handle it.

▶

"I WISH WE could do a real location shoot," Rei says as she plops down next to Kosaka to touch up her makeup. "In Okinawa, maybe. Even Atami would be nice."

"Didn't you have beach shots in your first photobook?" Aimi asks. At Rei's look of surprise she blushes. "I saw a copy in the office."

"You know where we shot those?" Rei doesn't wait for Aimi to take a guess. "Odaiba! That's why I was standing on the rocks. There's hardly any real sand. And then I cut my foot on some glass and Kosaka had to carry me back to the car. It hurt so much."

"Maybe for your third photobook," Kosaka says.

"I bet it'd sell really well, though. Everyone loves swimsuit shots."

The studio that Hiyoko PRO has rented out for the day has seven floors of sets above the cycloramas: classrooms, libraries, bedrooms, fake kitchens and bathrooms, even a corner made up to look like a church. The girls pose in casual clothes on a fake street corner and wear white sundresses in plastic gardens. Kosaka directs Mr. Hayasaka and the girls away from anything he deems too fanciful, though Aimi looks longingly at the spaceship bridge as they pass it.

"I can't believe I'm already getting a photobook," Aimi says.

"It's easier this way," Kosaka says. "We'll wait to release it after your second single comes out. But since we have Mr. Hayasaka booked for the day, we should make the most of it."

The building is all theirs, so Rei and Aimi don't waste time going back to the locker room to change. They duck around corners or behind set dividers to wriggle into different outfits. Mr. Hayasaka's assistant carries their suitcases full of costumes. Rei considers asking her name, but Mr. Hayasaka goes through assistants so fast that it hardly matters. This girl is taller than the last one, a little freckled, a little standoffish in a way that Rei parses as vague contempt.

Once she's changed into her next outfit Rei steps back into the kitchen set. Aimi claps a hand over her own mouth, doing nothing to muffle her "Wow!"

Rei has dressed exactly to the specifications of the shoot plan: a men's white button-down, long enough to skim the tops of her thighs, half-buttoned over a baby blue lace underwear set. The shoulder coverage makes the whole getup, by cubic inches of skin exposed, slightly more modest than the pajamas she shot in half an hour ago.

She sucks in her cheeks as if this can prevent her blushing under Kosaka's cold scrutiny. He steps in close to tousle her hair, pulling a curl down into the open collar of her shirt to draw the eye towards her cleavage and fluffing her roots for volume.

"Good," he says. "Hayasaka, what do you think?"

"Perfect," Hayasaka agrees. "Start with the coffeemaker, Rei."

There are an array of fake appliances in the kitchen, and Mr. Hayasaka coaches her through her poses. She pantomimes making coffee, then perches on the kitchen counter with the mug cradled in her hands: Soft Café Nymphette, the morning after. She holds up a bottle of wine and a corkscrew. She pretends to wash the dishes. She leans over the counter to allow a peek at her bra; she rests her back against the fake refrigerator, feet just slightly apart, and bites her pouting lip for the camera. Neither Kosaka and Mr. Hayasaka direct her to do anything overtly sexual, but Rei is perfectly aware of the fantasy she is catering to: the girlfriend experience, the idol domesticated and made one's own. When they call a halt she gratefully does up the rest of the buttons on the shirt and shimmies into a pair of jeans to cover up.

The group troops down the hall to a fake classroom where Aimi poses in a cosplay uniform, school emblem replaced with the Hiyoko PRO logo, on and around the desks: gazing wistfully out the window as though she's daydreaming through class, leaning flirtatiously against the edge of a desk; standing on her tiptoes to write on the blackboard so that her skirt rides up her thighs.

Rei and Ririko had aged out of this particular act before their debut. The sole Venus Versus photobook is full of sleepover shots: Ririko and Rei in skimpy matching pajamas, painting each others' nails and having pillow fights and nestling close together amid mountains of cushions. That staged look into the secret universe of best friends is a very specific sort of fantasy. She is glad that Kosaka has not asked her to try it with Aimi.

"That skirt is too long," Kosaka muses aloud. "Aimi, roll up your waistband. Twice should do it."

Rei is certain that she is not the only one who sees the flash of worry in Aimi's wide eyes. "Are you marketing her as a delinquent?" she asks. "Aimi looks fine the way she is."

"She has marketable legs," Kosaka says. "The fans will want to see them. Aimi, don't keep Mr. Hayasaka waiting."

Aimi nods and silently rolls her skirt up, exposing a few more centimeters of pale, soft thigh. She meets Rei's eyes, and Rei tries to smile despite her fury. Aimi has been on TV once! How many fans can she possibly have to demand this?

Aimi's answering smile is shaky but she keeps her eyes on Rei as Mr. Hayasaka clicks away and the freckled assistant sets up a fan on a desk in front of Aimi to blow her skirt back, outlining the gap between her thighs.

When Aimi is finally allowed to step away, Rei meets her.at the side of the room. "How are you feeling?" she asks, conscious of all the ears around them. "It's pretty intense, right? I remember being scared at my first shoot, too! But you'll get more comfortable with it."

"I'm fine," Aimi says. Her lip is red where she's chewed it. "It's—it's fun!"

Rei steps closer under the pretext of straightening Aimi's sidelocks. Aimi leans in, breathing loud and ragged, but if she's going to tough it out, it's not Rei's place to call her on it.

"Let's give the bedroom set another try," Kosaka says. He squats in the corner, laptop on his knees, reviewing earlier photos. "These shots of Rei aren't quite what her fans will want."

They march back up to the fifth floor, where a white wrought-iron bed decked in frothy blankets waits. Rei changes back into pajama shorts and a tank top and obediently kneels, lounges, sprawls as she is directed. Mr. Hayasaka tells her to "make herself comfortable" and she takes the cue for what it is, rolling onto her side to make her chest look bigger, stretching her arms over her head, sucking in her stomach before Kosaka has to remind her. She bats her eyelash extensions at the camera. Does it still count as exploitation when she's picking her own poses? She'd rather pretend it doesn't.

She cycles through her poses again, rolling around until the sheets are in disarray. This mattress is softer than her futon at home. The blankets are cheap, scratchy, trimmed with eyelet lace. Rei focuses on these things to block out the sound of Kosaka and Mr. Hayasaka discussing her body, which parts of it ought to be slimmed or recolored to make her more appealing.

Still, when at last they deem her performance satisfactory and let her leave the set, she is flattered by the way Aimi grabs her arm and whispers, "You looked really good."

The bedroom set chosen for Aimi is decked in pastels, a bed with a wooden headboard piled high with pillows shaped like macarons and biscuits. She hides around the corner to change and blot her makeup as Mr. Hayasaka resets his tripod.

"Rei?" Aimi calls out. "Can you help me with this?"

Rei ducks around the edge of the divider to find Aimi in a gauzy white babydoll, blushing furiously. The halter neck is tied in a neat bow but the fabric sags around her chest.

"I can't get the hooks to fasten," Aimi hisses. She presents her back to Rei, the bra-style hooks hanging open. Rei does them up and turns Aimi by the shoulders to face her again.

"Listen," she whispers. "Is this okay? You don't have to do anything that makes you uncomfortable."

"It's fine." Aimi lifts her chin. "This is what the fans want to see, right? It's what sells? So I can do it."

Rei's stomach crashes. She has not set a good example at all. She follows Aimi back to the set and watches the girl assume a slumber-party sprawl on the bed, lying on her stomach with her chin propped in her hands and her dainty white feet kicked up behind her.

Kosaka is standing at the side of the set, his critical eyes fixed on Aimi. Rei goes to him and leans into his side, conscious that she is still in the pajamas he chose for her. She looks up at him with her softest expression. "Don't you think that's an awfully risque costume for a high schooler?" she asks, keeping her voice low.

"We'll keep it tasteful," he reassures her. Rei does not know how to protest that they have already crossed the boundary of good taste without starting some debate about the age of consent versus the age of majority or about the necessity of winning fans by any means necessary. She paces to keep herself in Aimi's line of sight, refusing to change out of her pajamas as if in solidarity with the younger girl. She watches Aimi blush and fidget as she follows directions to lift her hem just a little, to prop up her chest with crossed arms, to smile. When Rei had done this with Ririko they'd giggled as they twined their legs together and cuddled close, treating it like a parody. But all this—it's played too straight for comfort.

When at last Mr. Hayasaka says, "I think that should be enough," Aimi is spread on her back, her head dangling over the edge of the bed. She bolts upright as if she is waking from a nightmare.

Rei darts forward but Kosaka has already stepped in to drape his blazer over Aimi's bare shoulders.

THEY FINISH UP the shoot too late to catch the last train home so Kosaka drives them. Aimi unbuckles her seatbelt to scoot closer to Rei and rests her head on Rei's shoulder. Rei slips her arm around Aimi, who stifles a yawn.

"You worked really hard today," Rei murmurs, choosing her words carefully. "Good job."

"You know, Aimi, you remind me of Rei when she was just starting out," Kosaka says.

"What?" Rei protests. "No, I was never this cute!" Aimi hums, pleased, and tucks herself more closely against Rei.

"You were very obedient, Rei. Eager to please."

"I'm still those things!"

Kosaka indicates his disagreement with an expressive silence. Aimi rushes to fill it.

"Was it hard going solo after you started in a unit?" she asks. "I'd be scared, doing something like that. I think you must be really brave."

There is a clear right answer, even if it's not the true one. "It wasn't hard. It's not like I was alone, after all. Mr. Kosaka was with me the whole time. There was nothing to be scared of, because I could rely on him." Three years together have taught her how to read his pleasure in how his shoulders relax against the driver's seat and in the rate of his breathing. Rei might be—probably is—more in tune with Kosaka, his shifting moods and irritations, than she ever was with Ririko. The thought might be the loneliest one she's ever had.

She strokes Aimi's silky hair and tries to remember what it felt like to curl Ririko's hair, taming the short crop to frame Ririko's heart-shaped face. The heat of the iron, the heat of her skin. Ririko always kept her eyes open when Rei styled her hair, watching as though she'd never seen a more fascinating show.

"What was Ririko like, anyway?" Aimi asks, her voice cloudy with drowsiness.

The answer is so big that it sticks in Rei's throat. Finally she says, "She was a great singer. I work so hard at lessons, but I still don't have her range. Or her vibrato—mine is pretty shallow, it's just chirimen vibrato. It's not very precise. Ririko had a lot more control than I do."

"But what was she like?"

She's gone forever, Ririko doesn't say. When I was finally brave enough to reach for her she wasn't there anymore.

"She had to back up her school notes on a cloud drive because she lost her notebooks so often, but she always shared the files with me. And she stole the wieners from my lunchbox, but only on days I cut them into octopi, because that shape tastes best. When we went for burgers after school she used more ketchup on her fries than anyone else I've ever known. She fidgeted whenever I did her eyeliner so I always had to clean up the line with a cotton swab."

"She'd always stay perfectly calm when she was lying," Kosaka cuts in. "She didn't take directions as well as either of you, so her photo shoots would run overtime. She argued with me about the costumes before her first mini-live."

"I don't remember that at all," Ririko says.

"You must not have been paying attention. She acted as if every idea she'd ever had was special and important just because it was hers, with no respect for anyone else's market research or expertise." Perhaps he realizes how loud his voice has grown in the confines of the car, because he abruptly relents. "But she was a good singer. Not cut out for being an idol, but a good singer."

When he brakes for a stoplight he glances back at Rei, his expression fond.

"You're not like her, Rei," he says. "I can trust you."

What a coward, using divide-and-conquer tactics against a ghost. Rei knows she is meant to be grateful. She is supposed to smile back and promise that she will always be obedient and lovable and unlike Ririko.

But she holds her plan within her like a small, fragile bauble, hoping that by singing her own "Hybrid Heart" she will show him that her ideas are worth something, that she too can make things others want. And best of all, this time she's making something she likes too.

She is more like Ririko than he knows.

Rei feigns a yawn of her own, stretching, jostling Aimi from her shoulder. "Does that mean I'll get schedule emails too?"

The air pulls taut between them.

Before it can snap, Aimi says, "I'm really nervous about filming the PV for my first single next week!"

There: the lines are drawn. Aimi may not understand that she has shown her hand, but Rei will remember. If Aimi senses that Kosaka is uncomfortable she will give him an out.

How many times has Rei done the same? No
wonder Ririko kept her secrets so close. She wasn't the
peacekeeper that Rei and Aimi are. Does Kosaka pick
appeasers on purpose, or do they mold themselves to fit
him? Neither option speaks well of anyone in this car.

"Really?" Rei asks, unwilling to let Aimi's words hang.
She doesn't deserve silence. "You're going to have so much
fun! I remember I was really happy when I got to film my
first PV."

"It's going to be Cinderella-themed. With a dress, and
horses, and everything." Passing headlights illuminate
Aimi's smile. She's so happy to be playing dress-up in
Yukarin's branding that it would be cruel for Rei to point
out the unoriginality. "Will you play my fairy godmother
in the video? Mr. Kosaka said I could ask you."

The contrast is pathetic. Rei couldn't even stand up
for Aimi today when she was scared, much less make any
wishes come true. She is not a real witch—because isn't a
fairy godmother just a witch judged socially acceptable—
but maybe pretending for a little while would feel better
than the jail of being a princess.

"Of course," she says as Kosaka pulls up outside her
apartment building. "I'd be happy to."

Kosaka turns back to look at her as he unlocks the
car door. "Sleep well," he says. "Don't forget, you have
rehearsal tomorrow."

To have forgotten necessitates having been told in the
first place, but Rei will take even this imitation of an olive
branch. "Looking forward to it," she says.

Kosaka idles the car until he's seen her pass through the
autolock and into the lobby's single elevator. As Rei rises
towards her room she wonders what poison he might be
pouring in Aimi's ear.

▶

ALL THAT REI has ever been allowed to know in advance about her schedule is the dates, times, and locations of her concerts. After all, the ticket presale links are reposted on her social scroll no fewer than three times daily. In the weeks before the next one, she steps more carefully, says less, even to Aimi. Compliance is her sharpest weapon in self-defense. She hopes that this is enough to set a good example for the girl.

Her rehearsals move from the practice studio to Pacifico Yokohama itself two days before the show. With one day to go, she knows today will be her full dress rehearsal; all hands on deck to button and zip and blow-dry her to perfection. The costumes are never as nice up-close as they look from a distance: she shines, but she itches under all that glitter.

She paces the stage, gazes up to the balcony seats, hopes her smile makes it all the way to the last row. The cameras feed her face back into the giant screens flanking her as she ascends to the upper tier of the stairs in the center of the stage. She will start here, her voice slicing through the sweaty quiet of the waiting crowd, and then the guitars will scream to life below her. She imagines the cool gaze she will sweep across the room, letting her fans tell themselves she's making eye contact with *me, yeah, she looked right at me!* And then, when they feel seen, when they're waiting for her verdict, the smile will break slow across her face.

The audience will cheer for her and she will be safely distant on her glittering stage.

"From the day the world began, I knew that we would meet here," she sings, and revels in her voice rising to the rafters. The stage under her feet is shaking with the force of her song. Rei wonders if maybe she couldn't bring this whole building down, sing the entire waterfront to rubble and dust.

She's dancing through the bridge when Kosaka's voice fills the speakers.

"Start it over."

Rei doesn't stumble, though it takes two more steps for her to stop; her weight is balanced too far to her left. She straightens her spine, centers her weight, and looks dead ahead to the control booth near the back of the first tier of seating.

"Do you want me to do something differently?" she asks, her miked voice echoing like thunder.

"I told you to start over, didn't I?" he snaps. She turns to the musicians at the side of the stage and bows an apology for wasting their time.

His voice, booming behind her, softens slightly. "This time, smile for the back row."

He can't have stopped her just for that! That's not worth interrupting the musicians for; that's the kind of note you give at the end of the song.

She heads for position zero at the top of the stairs, the little masking tape "T" that tells her where to stand, and starts over.

This time Kosaka lets her get through two songs before he stops her. Her arm movements aren't sharp or forceful enough. She nods meek assent, and when she tries again she flings her arm out so hard that she feels her shoulder seize up.

When her fourth song ends he rewards her with what could almost pass for praise: "Why can't you do that every time?"

Rei doesn't know what he's objecting to, but every time he yells at her he drags her back from that pure and untouchable place that feels like the source of all sound. By the end of the first act, she's ready to drop, exhausted by the emotions pushing and pulling her: the calm of accepting direction, the anxiety and the itchy, claustrophobic pressure of trying to please.

The second act is no better. Kosaka criticizes everything from the timbre of her voice to the fit of her costumes, getting in a few mean jabs about her recent grocery purchases, then just as abruptly praising the graceful curve of an outswept arm or the pose she strikes at the end of a song.

Three more songs and then she can rest, Rei tells herself. She only needs to make it through the encore now. Three more songs and then she can go home and cry.

But that's not true at all, is it? Three more songs, and then the choreographer will have notes for her, the costume fitter will strip her, and she will have to take her hair down and wipe off her makeup while Kosaka continues to flip hot or cold, sugar or sour. She thinks of the hands that will be on her, today and tomorrow: an idol is a shared good, a public resource. No one touches her anymore except to take from her—to fix her to their liking or else to get their fix of her.

It's not worth it. Was it ever worth it? She wants to go home and fall into a century of sleep.

It was easier with Ririko, when they'd been able to feed off each other's energy: darting glances at each other in the mirror while they did each other's hair and makeup, high-fiving as their paths crossed in the middle of the stage. Every song felt like they were getting away with something. How had they tricked the world into watching them, worshiping them, like they deserved it?

Ririko had always treated the stage like it existed just for her, even when it was just the patterned linoleum of the mall. When they'd marched out into the little square in the center of Sunshine City, their first and worst venue, Rei had been terrified of the handful of bored looky-loos hanging over the railings, staring down from the three floors of shops above them. She could tell just by their expressions that they had no idea who Venus Versus was; they'd only been attracted by the commotion. But Ririko had just tapped her toe on the linoleum three times, sinking herself into the rhythm, and started singing like every shopper was there to see her.

And precisely because Ririko had that fearlessness, Rei could follow her out, sing her lines, dance a cautious distance away from the fountain behind them that was just high enough to trip on. She could smile and wave, and when they were done and Kosaka was driving them back to the office, she didn't even shake from all the leftover adrenaline.

These days she feels like some part of her, deep inside, is shaking all the time.

"ONE, TWO, THREE, four—ugh, start over!" Rei snapped, but there was no heat in her voice. She fought her giggles back. "Ririko, I think it's—you're moving your arms too fast? And you need to pay attention to how you use your elbow. Articulate through the whole movement. You need to control it more or it looks all rubbery."

"None of that *means* anything," Ririko complained. She was smiling too. "Show me again?"

Their school was the tallest building for some blocks, and here their rooftop was all sunlight and bright sharp breeze sticking flyaway hairs in their lipgloss. Rei tilted her face towards the sun, basking in it, protected by a veil of SPF 120 Biore. "Like this."

She swept her arm grandly to the side, curled it in a graceful arc over her head, and brought it slowly down until her hand was extended, beseeching, towards an imaginary audience. "See, you need tension in your wrist, or the motion looks too loose. And you go slowly, because it has to match the long note at the end of the C-melo. Your hand can't be fully extended until the very last beat, and then you drop your fingers just a little to show your palm. That's the part everyone will want to take screencaps of, because you'll look so sincere and vulnerable."

"We'll *look* sincere and vulnerable," Ririko repeated with a laugh. "But we won't be, not really. Right?"

Rei grinned. "Only if they deserve it."

SHE'S OPENING WITH "Summer Shadows," starting it alone before the band kicks in. She loves starting songs a capella; something feels so intimate about it, even in big venues. When the bass kicks in it vibrates up through her toes, shaking her into action.

The lights are too bright and the crowd is too far away for her to see any faces: just how she likes it best. Kosaka can't interrupt her now that she's live. She is untouchably remote now, a tiny glittering island in the midst of a screaming ocean. The penlights and cyalumes are all glowing blue, and she yells greetings and thank-yous between songs, buoyed by the indistinct roar of approval.

And still she can't turn off her mind, always calculating: where to turn, which camera to play to, which arch expression or wide-eyed smile will sell the moment. Is now the right time to drop to her knees mid-song, arms outstretched to show the crowd she's overwhelmed with gratitude? If she turns her mic towards the audience, will they be ready to sing the refrain back at her? What emotions do they want to see, and which ones can she stand to give up to them?

When she pulls into the home stretch she's armed with the songs that will build the most hype, end the concert on a high note.

She's been fighting with Kosaka over where "Hybrid Heart" fit into the set list ever since she got the demo track. She wanted it in the encore, where people would go home humming it. He insisted that encores are for fan favorites, and it had to go into the body of the show. He wouldn't even let her end the main show with it so that the audience has time to process; he decided they'd close on "Mirror Fracture" so that her costume change between the second act and encore would reference Entropy Fighter Mizuki's redesign. Rei feels like she'll never get out of the shadow of Mizuki at this rate, but settles for second-to-last.

"I've been waiting to share something special with you. Do you want to hear my new single?" She giggles into the mic, and is gratified by the roar that meets her. "This one is called 'Hybrid Heart.'"

The anticipation raises goosebumps on her forearms; she doesn't know if the feeling is hers, or the audience's.

Rei knows she's supposed to say more. She's supposed to talk about what it means to her, to invite them in to marvel at her hopes and dreams. That's what an MC segment is about: cutting your own heart open like a butterflied steak so that the audience can see what's inside. But can her performance be worth anything if she has to explain it? Shouldn't it speak for itself?

She turns and meets the eye of her bandmaster at the keyboard. They nod at the same moment, caught in strange sympathy, and the music begins.

Generously, she sings the first verse as it's written; being sleepless on a rainy night isn't an experience exclusive to the tediously lovelorn. It's only when she's building up to the refrain that she begins to use her own words, ignoring Kosaka shouting venom in her earpiece. The chorus kicks in and she unravels her feelings, begging to know whether her song echoes in your bones.

She is answered abruptly when Kosaka cuts her mic.

Rei keeps singing, keeps moving, because she's been taught to keep going in case of technical difficulties, but she knows it doesn't matter; no one will hear her over the wail of the guitar and keyboard. When Kosaka turns her microphone back on at the end of the song, she apologizes to the audience, chastened, and promises that they'll hear the whole thing soon. He's snarling in her ear but she can't even distinguish the words. Her head is spinning as she moves into the final song. How could she have called this one so wrong? She'd thought that if it was a live show, if the fans' experience was riding on it, Kosaka would let her have her way and just find some petty way to punish her later. She'd made peace with that outcome when she planned this trick.

She knows now with awful clarity: if ever she stands on the Budokan stage, if ever she sells out the Tokyo Dome, it will be Kosaka's victory, not hers. She will only seize these treasures if she can carve away enough of herself to fit into him. And right there, her bitter steps keeping time for her sugar song, Rei finally chooses herself.

Tonight, on the Pacifico stage, is the last time her fans will see her face.

This resolve carries her through the end of the song and into the darkness that follows, allows her to suffer the hands stuffing her into her mycopleather-and-tulle Mizuki dress. Electric tube lights have been fastened over the seams to illuminate the lines of her silhouette. Yet more hands add clips to her hair, tiny faceted LEDs sinking into her long curls. She glows like a first-magnitude star.

The buzz of the audience fills the pitch black of Pacifico Yokohama. Gradually, the drone resolves into a chant. Rei catches her name in the din and holds back tears.

When the lights come up again she has perched herself halfway up the staircase, a lonely singularity caught between the upper and lower tiers of the stage. She can't see past the cocoon of lights to the great breathing void beyond her halo of soft white and blue. She lets herself make believe she's alone, watches the dust motes fall around her, and listens to someone else's words in her mouth. For all the singing she does about pure feelings, she's pretty sure she's never had one.

But she pretends so beautifully that right now, her voice reaching the rafters, she could fool even herself.

When the encore is over, when she has said her thank-yous and taken her bows, an odd tranquility seizes her. Rei poured out everything on this stage tonight, and Kosaka ruined it. He'd silenced the first honest thing she'd sung to them. She has spent so long binarizing her desires: responsible or not, respectful of her fans' time and money and emotional investment or not. She had believed that Kosaka thought the same way, but she sees now that the boxes into which he categorizes his options must be simpler than she knew: *in control* or *not*.

Empty, she drifts into the dull humming fluorescent light backstage. Kosaka runs to her and Rei goes still. She doesn't look at the cameras capturing backstage footage for her NeuroDouga channel, but she projects her voice to make sure they'll catch this. It doesn't matter that they'll edit it out before the video is posted. Right now she wants to be heard.

"Stay away from me."

Tears spring to Kosaka's eyes and Rei doesn't care if they're real. He can cry. She's done comforting him.

She calls her own cab.

A TENSE HOUR later Rei is ensconced in the back room of Bar Melos, a thin tin mug of cold vodka clutched in her clammy hands.

She spent most of the ride back to Tokyo watching out the window to be sure Kosaka wasn't following her, anxiety mounting with every tick of the meter. She had hesitated with her smart in one hand, knowing that it was broadcasting her location, still fretting over what to tell Aimi.

In the end her ping only said, "I'm sorry I couldn't be your fairy godmother. Good luck." As soon as the message was delivered, she factory reset her smart without waiting for a reply.

By the time the cab dropped her in Electric Town, the humidity had resolved into haze. Rei threaded through the crowds clogging the sidewalks, navigating by the glowing signs: here a yellow board proclaiming that Bar Anglerfish is open til 25:00; there a maid-cafe-slash-casino, its animated sign flashing a spill of poker chips; over there her own face on a poster outside a pachinko parlor.

And now Rei stares down a bartender whom she is sure is only pretending not to recognize her. This is Akihabara, after all, where her bromides are sold in every other store and her face beams from giant lectro-ads on the UDX screen at regular intervals.

"You don't have to tell me who you are or anything," Sasami says. "But I can't tell what you need just by looking, so..."

"There's a transmitter in my arm," she says. "And bioapps all over my brain, measuring my sleep, and how much and what I eat, and probably other things besides. It's all reported back to my manager." The word feels strange in her mouth. At some point, Kosaka became something bigger than a manager to her, maybe even bigger than a person, binding her with all his moods and all his rules and all his power to watch her from afar. But *idol* is a job, not a holy calling. "Well, I mean, he's not anymore. I just quit and I can't go back to have it all uninstalled, so—"

"Shh, it's okay." Sasami lifts tangles of wires and electrodes from a cardboard box on the desk.

"Can you take it out?" Rei asks. "Will it hurt?" Maybe that's what the vodka is for. On her worst days she's thought about doing it herself, with the little paring knife she uses to peel carrots and potatoes, but this is a pain—perhaps the only one—she's too afraid to inflict on herself.

"I can't cut your transmitter out, but I can fry it. Make it stop sending out a signal," Sasami says. "As for the bioapps...I'll have a look. No promises."

It's like a checkup with the doctor: reminders to take deep breaths and cold conductive gel swabbed onto her forehead by deft gloved hands. But this time, Rei's asked for it. She walked into this bar, where the glowing sign had been marked with the sigil that indicated biohacking service available, and she asked for help. Rei pulls measured breaths and does not shy away from Sasami's touch. She can hear laughter from neighboring bars through the walls and someone singing karaoke on the floor above them, and these things are comforting somehow. Her fingers have gone numb around the mug but she doesn't dare take a sip yet, not as long as Kosaka is still getting notifications from her body.

She closes her eyes against it but cannot stave off the flood of bitterness. Her traitorous body, tattling on itself. Her treacherous ambition, signing away her sovereignty with a fistful of consent forms. How did she ever fool herself into thinking she was in control?

"Oh," Sasami says, and then again, *"Oh."* Rei looks to find the computer screen alive and glowing as Sasami reviews everything in her: apps, patches, wetware updates. Over half of them are labeled *Hiyoko PRO Proprietary Program*.

Rei braces herself, waiting for Sasami to say her name. Their introductions had been noticeably one-sided, after all. What Sasami says instead is, "Do you want to talk about it?"

"No." The word comes out too much like a whimper for Rei's comfort.

"Okay. That's fine. I'll do what I can."

She scrambles the transmitter first, holding a little emitter shaped like a travel-size hairdryer up to Rei's bicep, moving and shifting to attack from all angles. Rei is sure that the way her arm grows sunburn-warm under the little ray gun is a purely psychosomatic discomfort, but she feels herself starting to sweat a bit anyway. One of the graphs on the computer flatlines.

"Packet transmission via eighth-generation network is down to zero," Sasami says. "I think you could try to have a drink now, if you want."

Rei has read every clause of her contract backwards and forwards; she knows exactly what actions will cause her immediate termination as a Hiyoko PRO employee. Disabling her transmitter is the first of them.

She also knows that they can technically sue her for damages incurred as a result of her breach of contract. They can try, anyway. They didn't pay her enough to make her worth suing.

Rei's cheeks are hot as she takes a tiny sip of the vodka, her eyes riveted on the computer. Three different notifications burst into her field of view but the packet transmission monitor doesn't fluctuate.

"Good," Sasami says, satisfied. "That was the easy part, actually, but it's what makes the most difference."

Rei, smiling back up at her with a burning mouth, understands now that vodka will always taste like freedom.

The bioapps themselves require authorization codes, unknown to Rei, to remove. Cracking the codes without access to a company server, Sasami says, isn't impossible, but it might take days. She deletes the updates and patches instead, patiently rolling all Rei's wetware back to its original install state and reinstalling an adblocker. Kosaka had removed hers when he set up her social accounts on the premise that she needed to know what commercials other idols turned up in.

Who did this for Ririko, if anyone? Did Hiyoko **PRO** send a doctor to her apartment to disable all her wetware? Did she go to a backroom biohacker like this to sort things out? Or is she living with all the same pings and popups even now? Rei shudders a little at the thought that Ririko's body might still be reporting back to Kosaka, that he might still be monitoring her.

It will never be perfect. Some people's scars are visible as stripey keloid; Rei's scars come in the form of popup windows hovering in her vision to chide her about her calorie intake. But she's going to have to live around it somehow.

She pays cash, emptying her wallet into Sasami's hand, and smiles at the suggestion that she come back for a drink sometime. Maybe she will.

捌

IT **IS PAST** midnight when Rei returns to her apartment, a bryovinyl bag swinging from her wrist. She's so tired she can barely stand, and she can't sleep yet.

Vodka roiling in her empty stomach, she turns on the gas konro in the corner and evaluates her six-mat room while she waits for the water to boil.

He did not build it or buy it, he has never set foot in it, but Kosaka's fingerprints are all over her apartment. He lives rent-free in every smart appliance pinging him notifications around the clock.

The screech of the kettle saves her from the wild desire to burn it all down. Rei's reason reasserts itself. It would be unfair to make all her neighbors homeless for one flash of vengeful joy.

She takes a deep, steadying breath and fixes herself one of the cup noodles she bought at the conbini on the way home. She hasn't had one of these since she signed with Hiyoko PRO; too much salt makes her bloated, and she doesn't photograph as well.

On her third bite, the popups explode into her vision, warning her against empty calories and late-night snacking. Begging her to preserve her health, when really all it means to preserve is her mass-market appeal. She blinks through them with bleary eyes. The growl in her stomach could be hunger, could be rage.

The noodles are a little limp, the curry broth gritty, and yet every bite is a celebration. Her tipsy haze recedes slightly. An undercooked pea catches in her molars. She laughs around a mouthful of noodles and rehydrated vegetable chips and knows that it's not this easy to get better, that she might trip into a pit of self-loathing and skip her meals tomorrow, that she might spend the rest of her life fighting all the subroutines programmed into her psyche. Knowing all that cannot rob her of this moment. Any ground gained, every step towards reclaiming herself, still feels like a victory.

She stands in her stuffy little room, eating her dinner a scalding gulp at a time, sobering up and marveling at herself. How long will this courage last?

Was this giddy wonder what Ririko felt, the first time she kissed a boy and walled off a secret corner of herself?

When the noodles are gone, she chugs the broth right from the flimsy cup, cumin and onion powder sticking clumpy to her tongue. Her stomach churns but her bare feet are firm on the imitation wood flooring, its wax worn thin and patchy. If she will carry on living here—and she must, because where else would she go?—she must evict Kosaka.

She takes her alarm clock off the wall and her blinds off the window, unscrews her shower head from the hose, and piles them on her tiny veranda. She can't bear carting them down to the communal trash bins right now. She unplugs her refrigerator and watches the lights indicating network connectivity wink out. Maybe if she doesn't open it, the food inside will stay cold until morning. Not that there's much in there.

She'll get a new fridge, she promises herself. A small one, because that's all she can afford—she'll have to hunt down one of the old-fashioned models that can't spy and tattle on her—and she'll pack it with things she wants to eat, things she's denied herself. What will it be like to eat for pleasure again regularly? Rei knows herself well enough to understand that her pleasure, for now, is still tainted with anxiety. It may be for a long time. But it's still something to look forward to.

The climate control unit mounted over the window gives her pause. She'd like to rip the thing right off the wall, even though she'll need to stand on a table to reach it. For tonight she unplugs it from the outlet. The night is sweltering but it won't hurt her to sleep with the window open. Tomorrow she can check the unit more thoroughly, make sure no backup battery is keeping it online. She won't be able to justify the expense of a new one. She'll learn to deal with the heat.

The smart futon is a trickier prospect. It's too expensive to replace, but Rei's unsure how to get the transmitter out without ruining it entirely. Just palpating the padding as she hunts for the transmitter and its solid-state battery makes the sweat prickle on the back of her neck. What is it telling Kosaka right now? Is he paying attention?

She has to stop to kneel over the toilet as her curry ramen makes an abrupt reappearance. She rinses her mouth, drinks a glass of water, breaks off a bite of the slightly stale CalorieMate in the cupboard to put something back in her stomach. Rei isn't going to swear off vodka entirely, but she vows to have a proper meal first next time.

She finds the transmitter near the foot of the futon, a box the size of a business card and as thick as the joint of her thumb. She cuts it out with a kitchen knife and drops it in a bowl of water, glad she'll be able to salvage the futon itself. She replaces the cover to hide the hole and spreads her quilt over the whole thing.

A spare towel goes over the window to grant her privacy in the absence of the blinds, and Rei surveys the domain that is newly hers. It feels alien, but when is the last time she felt safe? Would she recognize "safe," if she felt it? She's been under siege for so long that she's disoriented by its silent aftermath and the strange fact of her survival.

The frantic energy carrying her through this night drains away. It's normal to feel a little empty after a live, when the adrenaline fades and the happy rush of dopamine levels off. Going home to her small, quiet box of a room is usually such a dramatic contrast to a hall full of screaming fans that it leaves her itchy. But the restlessness she feels tonight is something different and new. Her future yawns before her like the white void of a cyclorama.

Maybe this is what passes for happiness.

The can of Yebisu in the fridge is months old, but unopened. Rei retrieves it once she's in her pajamas and sits cross-legged on her futon to crack it. Bitter hops and sweet malt dance on her overstimulated taste buds and useless notifications blink recriminations at her, but it leaves her feeling viciously satisfied. She will enjoy this, even if her body punishes her for it later, because she has earned it. She sips her beer slowly and lets her restless brain run wild.

She will defend herself. She will not yield her autonomy again. She will find a way to negotiate a truce with her body. Even in this buoyant mood, vowing to love herself feels a little too ambitious.

Rei has no idea how she will carry out any of these lofty goals, but she's determined to figure it out.

As she sprawls back onto her futon, one goal shines clearer than the rest. Tomorrow, she tells herself as she tries to wriggle into a comfortable position. Tomorrow she will rebirth herself. She will sing from behind an avatar, her interiority eliminated and thus protected, and she will keep singing until Ririko hears her.

▶

IT'S HARDER THAN it looks. The start of a song is humming in the back of her brain if only she can put it together, but she doesn't have the space to do so just yet: she needs to survive, first. Everything has a learning curve, and some are steeper than others.

Her days are her own, even as she drifts routineless through them, teaching herself to listen to her body. She sleeps when she is sleepy, eats when she is hungry. These things are probably common sense to other people, but she has spent so long denying and disciplining her unruly body that to her it is like learning a new language from some faraway country. She still gives herself stomachaches on the regular, her body utterly unused to processing whole meals, but gradually she notices that her sleep is sounder and her mind sharper on waking. Promising herself that nothing is forbidden anymore, she fights to remember pleasure in food: the salty gold of a raw egg on hot rice, mentaiko on spaghetti, mackerel simmered in miso. She will never eat another vitamin jelly or packet of bland sliced salad chicken again unless she actually wants to.

A new shower head is cheap enough but she can't afford a new climate control unit. Rei takes showers in the morning, and long cool baths at night to stave off the mugginess of summer. She still leaves the lights off when she's in the bath; looking too closely at her changing body sets off flares of vestigial panic that leave her shaking, unable to silence Kosaka's criticisms looping in her head. But in the dark she gently runs her hands over a stomach that is no longer concave and tells herself that she is okay. She tries to believe herself too.

She sells things online to make ends meet. Her closet is crammed full with her own memorabilia, posters and towels and bromides, all boxed up for sentimental safekeeping. She always thought she'd want these things so that she could look back on her career someday, show them off graciously in some retrospective documentary featurette, but it's surprisingly easy to let go of them. She signs everything before she lists it to raise the value.

She even sells gifts she's received from fans. Of course she never could have kept all of it herself. After every concert she and Kosaka would painstakingly sort through the bins into which her fans had dropped their tributes. Gifts of food and candy were passed on to the event staff; Rei usually wound up handing out any stuffed animals to them too, unable to care for such a huge menagerie. It had always been her prerogative, and often a necessary supplement to her income, to discreetly sell the handbags and jewelry that didn't suit her style. Now she purges even the things she liked enough to keep. Out of the public eye, she doesn't need to be fashion-conscious and photo-ready as much as she needs the security of cash in the bank.

She's glad to let go of her *Mizuki* merch, too: posters and clearfiles and pamphlets signed by the director and by Mizuki's speaking voice actor, a 1/7 scale figure still in the box, t-shirts she's never worn. They sell for higher prices than her own merch did, but she needs the money enough that she doesn't take it personally. The figure alone nets her half a month's rent.

Rebellion is the road that Ririko walked first, and as she follows, Rei sees the blurred afterimage of her friend lurking in every shadow. Those fleeting thoughts are somehow almost enough to ward off the loneliness of independence.

Rei attends to her rebirth slowly, pecking away at its different aspects every day like a chick testing every curve of its shell. The open source downloads are easy to find. All the software she needs is at her fingertips in the time it takes her to slurp down instant yakisoba, doing her best to to ignore the useless pinging of her calorie intake meter.

The time she spends designing her new avatar speaks more to her own indecision than to any difficulty with the interface. Rei knows what she looks like in the mirror, and what she looks like in photos, and where those two diverge. She doesn't edit herself as slim as Kosaka would have. She toggles the slider down so that her eyes aren't so cartoonishly huge. She tries to keep her pointy little chin, though. In the end, ZERO still looks an awful lot like Rei, but at least she doesn't look like Entropy Fighter Mizuki.

Over painstaking hours, she plunks out and refines a melody on her electronic keyboard, then fills it out with samples from open-access libraries. She stops sleeping for a while. She only realizes how long she's been awake when she plays back her track and realizes she's running two competing basslines. She likes it enough to keep it, though.

The street noise makes it hard to get a clean recording in her apartment. She sings in her futon in the dead of night, all the way under the covers, curled fetal around her microphone. Rei sneezes in the middle of her best take and has to discard a verse. Her second-best take has a snatch of a passing ambulance in it, but she can disguise that with some synthesizer noises.

She loses track of time. She hears the song even in her sleep now, her voice laid over drum loops and a hesitant shuffle of synth, promising *to make sense if only you'll keep listening. She could stand to keep living in this world as long as she's coaxing your heart to beat in time to her song, because she's here just for you.*

Putting it all together, making her doll dance, takes weeks. Rei knows the basics; it's only Avidance, after all. The interface has hardly changed and she still has muscle memory left over from all the time she and Ririko spent playing around with it in high school, dreaming of the idols they wanted to be instead of studying for entrance exams. But Avid's movement engine is better now, and more complex too. She watches tutorials on NeuroDouga, binges LYRICO's music videos to study how she moves.

Maybe the best thing about ZERO is that she can't push it or punish it the way she used to do herself. She can't tire it out, she can't hurt it. And if repetition doesn't teach either of them anything, then she can step away

sometimes. She can rest her eyes and her head and try
again in fifteen minutes. Rei had forgotten what that felt
like: that the body could be an oasis instead of a prison.

She learns again to take breaks. She watches music
videos and variety shows and tries to teach herself that
the featured talents are not her rivals. Aimi appears
during commercial breaks as the new face of Sunny Labo
cosmetics. She's smiling dazzlingly and her costume,
yellow and white and voluminously ruffled, suits her
perfectly, but Rei finally understands what Ririko meant
that day. She doesn't like the costume at all.

She hopes that Aimi will be satisfied with whatever she
achieves, that she won't wake up in a prison of her own
making. Despite everything, Rei wants to believe that
Aimi could be as happy as she looks on TV. Some part of
her, trained to give a man the benefit of the doubt, insists
that Kosaka could change, that all she's suffered was her
own fault. Rei brought out the worst in him, they were
bad for each other—but of course he's not a monster. Of
course he won't treat Aimi the same way.

Rei still has to tell herself that it was her own fault, so
that she can keep believing she had any agency at all.
There were a thousand points at which she could have
turned back, and refused. She'd rather take the blame
for how everything turned out than think of herself as a
victim.

ZERO, at least, will never have to pretend happiness.

Her work comes together slowly, words and notes
stacking up, syncing motion to sound a beat at a time. By
the end she isn't sure if it's actually good, if she's satisfied
with it or if she just wants to stop listening to her own
voice echoing in her dark apartment. Maybe it's ceased to
matter.

Rei starts the upload and waits. It would be nice, she
thinks, if her feelings reached Ririko.

ACKNOWLEDGMENTS

I would absolutely have fled into the woods in a fit of nerves if not for my agent, Jennifer Jackson, and my editor, dave ring. Thank you for convincing me that I should, just this once, allow myself to be perceived.

夏じるし先生へ、素敵な表紙を描いてくださって、誠にありがとうございます。ずっと大事にします!

My everlasting gratitude to the Clarion West class of 2017, without whom I would not be here today, who sat with me through a thousand dark lunches, who graciously read more drafts than should be expected of anyone.

To my Strange Friends (Brandon O'Brien, Jeoi Gawain Lin, Valerie Valdes, and Mike Underwood): Thank you for all our adventures, and thank you to Arv (Gregory A. Wilson) for giving us a platform from which to throw crickets.

Kisorie V.: Isn't it amazing how much we got done while we were waiting for the world to split open?

ねこ屋の皆さんへ、「感謝」という言葉で伝え切れない気持ちですが、これからもずっと 一緒に歌いましょう。
月曜日を輝かせてくれるりこむーんへ、感謝というより恩があります。和訳が出版された ら読んでください。
どんな曲でも調子を合わせてくれる守里先生へ、いつも元気に付き合ってくれていること はありがとうございます。
義弘へ：safe as houses.

一緒だから照らせる世界があるだと教えてくれたKTに、 共鳴をこめて。

ABOUT THE AUTHOR

Iori Kusano is an Asian American writer and Extremely Ordinary Office Gremlin living in Tokyo. They are a graduate of Clarion West 2017 and their fiction has previously appeared in *Apex Magazine*. Find them on Twitter @IoriKusano and Instagram as iori_stagram, or at kusanoiori.com.

ABOUT THE PRESS

Neon Hemlock is a Washington, DC-based small press publishing speculative fiction, rad zines and queer chapbooks. We punctuate our titles with oracle decks, occult ephemera and literary candles. Publishers Weekly once called us "the apex of queer speculative fiction publishing" and we're still beaming. Learn more about us at neonhemlock.com and on Twitter at @neonhemlock.